Fortune's Children™

Meet the Fortunes—three generations of a family with a legacy of wealth, influence and power. As they gather for a host of weddings, passionate new romances are ignited…and shocking family secrets are revealed…

JACK FORTUNE: When it comes to mergers and acquisitions, this millionaire doesn't miss *anything*. But will this new role as a single dad suddenly make him see *who* has been right under his nose?

AMANDA CORBAIN: For years this loyal secretary has had a hopeless crush on her charismatic boss. She's determined to fall out of love—until a special little girl enters Jack's life. And suddenly her Cinderella dreams *temporarily* become a living reality.

GRAY McGUIRE: This tough businessman only wants revenge on the Fortune family. And he's about to meet the perfect partner—Stuart Fortune's illegitimate daughter!

Fortune Family Tree

Caleb Fortune m. Lilah Dulaine

Stuart Fortune m. Marie Smith

Emmet Fortune m. Annie Mackenzie (d)

② GARRETT Fortune
—m.—
Renee Riley

④ MOLLIE SHAW**

③ JACK Fortune
—1st m.—
Sandra Alexander (d)
—b—
Lily Fortune
—2nd m.—
Amanda Corbain

① MACKENZIE Fortune
—m.—
Kelly Sinclair

Chad Fortune

⑤ CHLOE Fortune

Key:

① The Honour-Bound Groom
② Society Bride
③ The Secretary and the Millionaire
④ The Groom's Revenge
⑤ Undercover Groom

Symbols:

- - - - Affair
{ Twins
* Kate Fortune's brother-in-law
** Child of Affair

Fortune's
Children™

BRIDES

THE SECRETARY AND
THE MILLIONAIRE

Leanne Banks

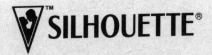

SILHOUETTE®

Silhouette and Colophon are registered trademarks of Harlequin Books S.A., used under licence.

First published in Great Britain 2000
Silhouette Books, Eton House, 18-24 Paradise Road,
Richmond, Surrey TW9 1SR

© Harlequin Books S.A. 1999

Special thanks and acknowledgement to
Leanne Banks for her contribution to the
FORTUNE'S CHILDREN: THE BRIDES series.

ISBN 0 373 76208 9

26-0005

Printed and bound in Spain
by Litografia Rosés S.A., Barcelona

This book is dedicated to all the hard-working secretaries who had a secret crush on their bosses.

LEANNE BANKS

is a number-one bestselling author of romance in the USA. She lives in her native Virginia with her husband and son and daughter. Recognised for both her sensual and humorous writing, Leanne likes creating a story with a few grins, a generous kick of sensuality and characters that hang around after the book is finished. Leanne believes romance readers are the best readers in the world because they understand that love is the greatest miracle of all. You can write to her at P.O. Box 1442, Midlothian, VA 23113, USA. An SAE with postage for a reply would be greatly appreciated.

Silhouette® is proud to present

Fortune's Children
BRIDES

Meet the Fortune brides: special women
who perpetuate a family legacy greater
than mere riches!

April 2000
A FORTUNE'S CHILDREN WEDDING:
THE HOODWINKED BRIDE
Barbara Boswell

THE HONOUR-BOUND GROOM
Jennifer Greene

May 2000
SOCIETY BRIDE
Elizabeth Bevarly

THE SECRETARY AND THE MILLIONAIRE
Leanne Banks

June 2000
THE GROOM'S REVENGE
Susan Crosby

UNDERCOVER GROOM
Merline Lovelace

**Remember, where there's a bride…
there's a *wedding*!**

Prologue

"When are you going to stop pining for Jack Fortune and get on with your life?" Carol Denton asked when Amanda rejected another blind date setup.

"I've tried dating other men. They all seem to be missing something."

Amanda Corbain knew Carol had a valid point, but she just couldn't get past her feelings for her boss, Jack. She glanced out the restaurant window at the busy Minneapolis downtown street and shrugged her shoulders. "Think about it," she said to her best friend. "Who can compare to Jack Fortune?"

"Okay," Carol conceded. "So he's blond, gorgeous, smart, wealthy and single. He's also your boss. He's a workaholic and commitmentphobic since his marriage busted up. Still changing women every three months?"

Amanda nodded glumly. "He's slowed down a little since his daughter came to live with him, but he still finds time to make the rounds." Unlike her, all of Jack's social partners were beautiful.

Carol gave a heavy sigh. "I hate to say this, but I think the man has ruined you."

Amanda felt a sinking sensation in the pit of her stomach. She didn't want that to be true. "He just can't seem to see me. As far as Jack is concerned, I may as well be the invisible woman." She took a sip of coffee and felt a surge of restlessness at the familiar lunchtime conversation topic. Whenever Carol asked about her progress with Jack, Amanda's answer was the same.

Carol made a face. "Have you ever thought about stripping off your clothes and sitting on his desk?"

"Yes," Amanda said without batting an eye. She'd envisioned such a scenario countless times. "But I'm not sure what I would do next. I think I might need remedial education in the feminine wiles department. Besides, I like my job, and my salary is helping put my sisters through college."

Carol finished her wine and shook her head. "It must be a burden to be such a responsible person. Were you ever impulsive? Even when you were a kid?"

Amanda thought of her father's death when she was very young. When Amanda had been just twenty years old, her mother's death had taken her family by surprise and she'd needed to hold everything together. "I didn't have much of a chance to be impulsive. The most impulsive thing I've done was accept the promotion with Fortune Corporation and move to Minneapolis from North Carolina.'' She smiled. ''A nineties Mary Tyler Moore.''

''You're going to have to do something,'' Carol told her. ''You can't spend the rest of your life staying home by yourself on Saturday nights and pining for Jack Fortune.''

''I know,'' Amanda said, putting the waiter's tip on the table as she prepared to return to work. ''I've got to find a way to stop being invisible.''

As soon as she got back to the office, Amanda poured a mug of hot black coffee and slid it onto Jack Fortune's desk ten seconds before he reached for it and automatically nodded his thanks. Listening to his smooth, baritone voice as he spoke with a potential client on the phone, she placed the faxes for his reference directly in front of him. He silently mouthed ''Thank you'' to her, another acknowledgment of her services.

Amanda wondered if he would choke on his coffee if she told him she would prefer a kiss, a nice long one. Turning her head, she rolled her eyes at herself. Better keep herself in check or her boss would learn she had a mile-high crush on him.

Jack always saw what she did and expressed appreciation in a dozen different ways. Yet he never ever seemed to see her. In a world filled with beautiful women, Amanda knew her appearance wouldn't stop traffic in Minneapolis or anywhere else. Her brown hair, brown eyes and average body made her the perfect unobtrusive assistant, or...invisible woman, she thought wryly.

''The demand for Fortune clothing has taken off,''

Jack Fortune said into the phone, glancing at the top fax. "Our profits are up thirty-eight percent, Bob. We have a new athletic wear line going head-to-head with the top designers. The retail market has had its shares of ups and down in the last few years. We'd like to give the customer a reason to come to your stores."

Crossing her arms over her chest, Amanda leaned against the doorjamb and stole a moment to listen to the sexy enthusiasm in his oh-so-persuasive tone. Jack's easy voice gave only a hint of the energy the man emanated.

His blond hair, startling green eyes and lean, muscular physique turned heads.

Amanda had never touched his hair. It wouldn't have been appropriate. That hadn't stopped her from wondering if his hair would feel crisp or soft against her fingers, She'd also wondered how his mouth would feel on hers. Hard, supple or both.

His personal sense of power, however, fit him better than his tailored suits. That dynamic power drew men's respect and caused women to make fools of themselves.

He was a conqueror, the corporate modern-day equivalent of Marco Polo. He was also a closer.

Yet he had a secret, tender side for his three-year-old daughter, Lilly. Amanda's heart softened at Jack's struggle to make Lilly feel at home. She wondered if he knew how seductive his tough and tender combination was.

He was a perceptive man, a demanding boss who inspired achievement and loyalty. Did he have any idea how many times his loyal assistant had fantasized about him making love to her on his big, cherry desk? Amanda knew Jack would never compromise his professional integrity with an office affair, but the familiar visual teased her all too often. Amanda pictured it happening after hours, during one of the many evening sessions she'd remained at work to help with a special project. The scene unfolded like a movie:

"Would you like coffee or a soda before you go home?" she asked Jack. *They'd been so focused on preparing the presentation they'd worked through dinner. His charcoal jacket hung on the back of his chair, his shirtsleeves were rolled up to reveal strong forearms, highlighted with the same blond hair that crowned his head.*

"A soda would work. Thanks," he said, then leaned back in his leather chair and stretched.

Averting her gaze from his, she left the room and grabbed his soda. On the way back, she pressed the icy can against her forehead, then pulled it away just before she entered his office.

She felt his gaze on her and knew she must be mistaken. Jack never really looked at her. He looked through her.

"There you go," she said and made herself smile. *"I'll see you in the morning for the Hartford presentation. Drive safely,"* she added and turned to leave.

"Amanda," Jack said, stopping her. *"Do you have plans tonight?"*

Her heart leaped, then she mentally smacked herself. He was just being polite. She turned back around and shook her head. "Nothing major." I just need to go home, she thought. I've been around you too long today, and I'm starting to have delusions that you might actually be seeing me as a woman instead of *just your assistant. "Have dinner with me," he said and stood. "You and I, we should talk."*

"Thank you, but I don't want to keep you out late with the presentation early in the morning. I know you've got that commute home."

"I'll be okay," he said with a slight grin that contrasted with his intent gaze. "We should talk."

As he walked toward her, she took a careful breath. "I—uh—"

He pressed his finger to her lips. "Just let me do the talking. You've been my secretary for four years now. I don't know why I've been so slow about this." *He tilted his head thoughtfully. "Maybe my rotten marriage. But that's over," he said. "I want you doing more than my paperwork. I want to take you to dinner. I want to see you after quitting time. I want to kiss you," he said, rubbing his thumb over her bottom lip. "But I can't take advantage of our business relationship. I want you to consider a transfer so I can see you personally. I need you," he said in a low, rough voice as he lowered his head. "I need you in my life."*

I need you. *Amanda's head was spinning. She'd dreamed of hearing those words from Jack.*

"Amanda, I need…"

The sound of Jack's voice jerked her out of her reverie, and she blinked at him.

"…the most recent sales projections for the Wyndham Retail Group." He glanced up at her and raised his eyebrows. "Problem?"

Amanda quickly shook her head. "No problem. I'll get them for you right away."

I need you. His words echoed inside her as she left

the room and took a mind-clearing breath. She could make a wish on every falling star that Jack would say those magic words to her about something other than office work. She could wish that he would need her the way a man needs a woman, but that would require him to see her. And as Amanda had learned, when it came to Jack Fortune, she might as well be the invisible woman.

One

***

"Amanda, I need you *now*." Jack said two days later.

Jack's words on Amanda's intercom kicked her heart into overdrive. Wincing at her overreaction, she put a calming hand to her throat. She'd rarely heard that tone from him, and never coupled with those exact words. "I'll be right there," she managed, and swiveled out of her chair.

She opened his office door to find him pacing, his long stride covering the generous width of his office. He stopped when she closed the door behind her.

"It's the housekeeper's day off. The nanny is sick," he told Amanda as he raked his hand through his hair. "I'm closing the Eastco deal today."

He walked toward her, and her stomach dipped. For Amanda, stomach dips, butterflies, accelerated heartbeats had become part and parcel of working for Jack. The challenge lay in not letting her feelings show.

"This isn't part of your job description, but I need someone I can count on to take care of Lilly now. Today. Will you do it?"

"Of course," she said, then gave a light laugh. He truly had no idea of all that she would do for him. "I thought you were going to ask something difficult."

He exhaled in relief and shook his head. "You're one hell of an assistant, Amanda. You can be sure I'll remember this at your next performance review," he told her.

Amanda felt a twinge at his professional tone. "That's not necessary. My experience taking care of my brother and sisters doesn't have much to do with my office performance."

"No. But in this case, it does with *mine.* I should warn you Lilly still hasn't adjusted to living with me."

"That's understandable," Amanda said, the slight nerves in his voice surprising her and grabbing at her heart. "Her mother hasn't been gone very long. Not even two months. That will change."

"God, I hope so," he muttered, returning to his desk. "The poor kid hides behind the furniture every time I enter the room. She barely knows me, since Sandra made it difficult for me to see her. The nanny I hired has impeccable references, but Lilly hasn't warmed to her." He frowned, then seemed to switch gears. "Use one of the company limos. As soon as the meeting is over, I'll come home."

Amanda nodded, hesitating before she said, "You

asked me to remind you about your dinner date with Ms. Sullivan.''

He frowned. ''I'll cancel.''

Amanda wrestled with her conscience. Trina Sullivan, a beautiful redhead, was Jack's current social partner. She swallowed her reluctance and envy in one gulp. ''You don't have to cancel. I can stay with Lilly tonight.''

He shook his head. ''No. I'll cancel.''

Amanda bit her tongue to keep from screaming with joy.

Thirty-five minutes later the nanny, pale and clearly ill, invited Amanda into the marble foyer, introduced her to Lilly, then disappeared to her upstairs bedroom.

Amanda looked down at the perfectly dressed three-year-old, tightly gripping a worn, stuffed one-eyed cat. Lilly's blond hair fell past her shoulders in tousled curls. The sorrow in her wide green eyes made Amanda's heart turn over.

She knelt in front of Lilly. ''I have a cat, too. Her name is Delilah. What's your cat's name?''

''Miss Annabelle,'' Lilly whispered.

Amanda's stomach twisted at the fear on her face. Lilly seemed such a tiny, forlorn figure especially in the grand surroundings of Jack's home. ''You wanna go outside for a while?''

Lilly nodded, and when Jack's daughter put her tiny hand in hers, Amanda's heart was lost.

Jack pulled his rain-splattered Mercedes into the tree-lined drive that led to his house. He was so preoccupied that he barely noticed how the warm, spring rain shower that had fallen on Minneapolis most of the afternoon, had made the green grounds of his estate even greener.

Jack was worried about Stuart. His father had been distracted lately. Profit figures looked great, but tension hung about Stuart like the thick humidity before a thunderstorm. Jack couldn't tell if Stuart's concerns were with the Fortune business or his own company, Knight Star Systems. Jack knew little about Knight Star Systems since he'd always felt a responsibility to make his mark at Fortune, especially since his brother, Garrett, had made it clear corporate life wasn't his bailiwick and had chosen ranching instead.

If that wasn't enough, although Jack was jazzed about the new account he'd just bagged, he was worried about Lilly. He had no idea what to do with her. Quiet and withdrawn, she hadn't even begun to warm to Ms. Brown, the nanny. She hadn't warmed to him, either, and that knowledge stung.

As he turned toward the garage, he glanced over the grounds and did a double take. He stopped the car and stared.

In an alcove of blooming trees beside his house, his secretary and his daughter were skipping through a mud puddle. He pressed the button to lower his window, and the sound of Lilly's laughter drifted through the air. His heart stopped. He couldn't remember when he'd last heard that sweet, wonderful sound.

Amanda's husky laughter joined with Lilly's. Getting out of the car, he gazed at his assistant. The rain had slowed to barely a sprinkle, but Amanda had clearly caught the worst of it. Her wet, fine hair hung limply to her shoulders. Her business suit clung to her slim curves, and her shoes and stockings were covered with mud.

Her face bright with pleasure, she didn't seem to give a damn that she was a complete mess. The movement of her body drew his gaze again. He noticed the subtle curves of her breasts and hips, her long shapely legs, and felt a tug of awareness. Clearly unaware of him, however, Amanda sang a chorus from ''Singin' in the Rain.'' Lilly pulled at Amanda's stockings, and they both laughed again. Amanda kicked off her shoes, and Jack watched in amazement as his painfully practical and conservative secretary briefly bared her thighs and ditched her nylons.

He felt the disconcerting tug of awareness again and swore under his breath. He'd never really thought of Amanda as a woman. He'd never really wanted to. After all, she was the best damn assistant he'd ever had and he was too driven with his goals for Fortune Corporation to want any distractions.

Sure, she had a few nice features more or less— big brown eyes and an easy smile. Her primary value to Jack, however, had always been her organizational skills and uncanny ability to anticipate his professional needs. Her professional skills would continue to be her primary value, he told himself. Suddenly conscious of the fact that he was standing in the rain staring at his secretary, he scowled, got back in his car and pulled into the garage.

Grabbing a large black umbrella, he walked toward

the two mud-splattered females. The bottom half of his daughter looked as if she'd been dipped in chocolate milk. Amanda caught sight of him and pointed out his presence to Lilly.

"I think I'm late with the umbrella," he said.

"We're a mess, aren't we," Amanda said, wincing, then she shrugged and chuckled. "You may not remember this, but when you're a kid, some days you just need to stomp in a mud puddle. Don't worry. I think I can get the mud out of her outfit."

"And yours?" he asked, his gaze inadvertently drawn to her damp blouse, which emphasized her small breasts and hardened nipples encased in lace. Feeling a slow, seductive curl of warmth in his stomach, he blinked and forced his gaze down to his daughter. Lilly was clinging to Amanda's leg. Hiding again. Jack sighed. Failure was an alien concept to him, but when he looked at his daughter, all his wins at work turned to dust.

"Dry cleaning works wonders," Amanda said, and turned to Lilly. "While you and I were playing in the mud, I bet your daddy bagged another big deal this afternoon."

Lilly looked at him with wide, solemn, unblinking green eyes.

"Hey, princess," he said, and gently touched her soft, damp cheek with his knuckles. "Did you have fun today?"

She nodded, but said nothing.

He glanced down at the bedraggled, stuffed cat she held in her hand. "We'll need to wash your kitty, too," Jack said, feeling, as he often did with his daughter, at a loss.

"Miss Annabelle," Lilly whispered.

His heart squeezed. Lilly rarely spoke, even in a whisper.

"Miss Annabelle needs a bath and you do, too," he said.

"'Manda says I get a cookie," Lilly whispered.

He glanced up at Amanda and raised his eyebrows. He wondered how she had won over his daughter so quickly.

"A cookie is a magical thing," Amanda told him, as if she could almost read his mind.

An hour later, after Jack pulled strings and got a doctor to examine the nanny, and Amanda gave Lilly a bath, he joined his assistant and daughter for a dinner of grilled cheese sandwiches and soup.

"I would have heated the casserole if I'd known about it," Amanda said. "Ms. Brown mentioned it when I took her soup to her room."

Noting the way his daughter gobbled down her sandwich instead of picking at her food the way she usually did, Jack shook his head. "No, this is fine. It was kind of you to feed us."

"Not exactly a celebration dinner," Amanda said with a wry smile.

"Celebration?" Jack repeated.

"For the Eastco account."

"How did you know I got it?"

She rolled her eyes. "As if they stood a chance."

He felt a curious rush of pleasure at her praise. "You're assuming I always win."

"Safe assumption. I've seen you in action," Amanda said, then turned to Lilly. "I think your dad deserves a cookie. What do you think?"

Lilly stared at him, then nodded at Amanda. "Can I please have another cookie?" she whispered.

Amanda gave a mock gasp. "Another cookie? But you've already had two today." She bent closer to Lilly. "Are you sure you're not a cookie monster in disguise?"

Lilly giggled, and the sound surprised Jack again. He gazed at Amanda and made a quick, instinctive decision. "It's getting late. Why don't you stay here tonight?"

Amanda did a double take and looked at Jack as if he'd sprouted horns. "I—I don't have any clothes for work tomorrow and—"

"I can take you by your apartment on the way to the office," Jack said, thinking he'd never seen her flustered.

She blinked. "And my cat," she managed. "I need—"

"Do you have a neighbor you can call?"

"Well, yes—"

"Good," Jack said, knowing he was railroading her. He hadn't seen his daughter this happy in weeks, and if Amanda was the magic potion, then he sure as hell didn't want her leaving yet. "Then it's settled. You probably want to get out of those wet clothes. I'll see if I can find something for you to put on after your bath."

He returned shortly with one of his terry robes and a pair of silk pajamas he'd never worn. When his wife Sandra had left two years ago, he'd gotten rid of every remaining article of clothing she'd left behind. He'd wanted no sign of her left in the house. She'd taken his name, his money and his daughter, and left him with bitter emptiness. Sandra might be dead, but the damage she'd caused continued.

The complete and utter sense of failure he'd felt at the time of the divorce echoed through him again as he watched Amanda with his Lilly through Lilly's open bedroom door.

Brooding, Jack absently noticed Amanda had climbed into Lilly's small bed with his daughter as she read and sang with her instead of sitting in the chair beside Lilly's bed as Ms. Brown did. After she finished *The Little Engine That Could* and a chorus of "Eensy Weensy Spider," Jack entered the room and kissed Lilly good-night.

Amanda left the door cracked and joined him in the hallway. "I think she's a goner."

"Are you sure you didn't miss your calling?" Jack asked her.

She met his gaze. "What do you mean?"

"You're so good with children. Did you ever think about working with them in some professional way?"

She gave a half smile and shook her head. "I got my experience the natural way. I had a younger brother and younger sisters. My father died when I was young, so my mother counted on me a lot. Then when my mother died, they needed me even more."

"I forgot about your family," he mused, wonder-

ing why he hadn't paid more attention. "I've noticed
the pictures on your desk, but you don't mention them
often."

"Oh, I love them all," Amanda said, her voice full
of affection. "Both my sisters received academic
scholarships to college, and my bother operates his
own successful home-remodeling business. I'm very
proud of them, so don't get me started," she warned
him. "I won't stop and I'll end up boring the boss to
death."

"I'm not bored," he told her. "Would you like a
nightcap before you turn in?"

Amanda hesitated, a flash of uncertainty sweeping
across her face. For a second he thought she might
refuse and felt a strange sting of disappointment.

"Thank you. That would be nice," she finally said,
and pulled the lapels of his robe closer together as
they walked toward the den.

"The robe swallows you."

"Uh—well—"

"You're not going to lie to be polite, are you?"

Amanda's cheeks bloomed with color. "Okay, yes,
it does. But it's not a problem. It's just for one night."

He headed for the bar on the other side of the room.
"What would you like to drink?"

"White wine," she said, sitting stiffly in an over-
stuffed chair. "I don't have a sophisticated palate.
One glass usually makes me sleepy." She gave an
earnest but strained smile. "You have a lovely
home."

"Thank you. The decorator was highly recommended," he said, placing the wineglass in her hand.

He'd had the entire house redone after his marriage broke up, but he didn't impart that information to Amanda. He noticed her toes were curled into the Oriental carpet and he wondered about her uneasiness.

She nodded. "Whoever it was did a nice job."

Silence followed. Despite her tension, her presence reminded him of background music. He studied her again. Her hair, still slightly damp from her shower, was pushed behind her ear on one side and curved over her cheek on the other. Her skin was fresh-scrubbed and glowing. The robe gaped slightly at the neck, revealing the gentle curve of her breast; and lower, where she crossed her legs, he saw one silky calf.

He glanced at her face again and something about the restlessness in her dark eyes was sexy to him. He took a quick drink of whiskey at the thought.

If women were music, then he always chose loud, showy numbers, the better to make him forget his marriage failure. Amanda was background music. Too soft, too gentle. With her, he would have time to think.

Strolling closer to her, he propped a hand on a cherry end-table and looked down at her. "You've worked for me for four years now. Why are you uneasy with me?" he asked.

She sucked in a quick breath of surprise and glanced away. "I'm not. Well, maybe I am," she said, running her sentences together. "It's a different situation. A little odd. I'm wearing your robe, caring for your daughter, drinking a glass of wine with you." She finally looked up at him. "It's not the office."

"As you were singing 'Eensy Weensy Spider' with my daughter, it occurred to me that aside from the fact that you are the best assistant I've ever had, I don't know much about you."

She nervously brushed her hand against her neck. "There's not much to know," she said, and when he didn't fill the silence, added, "I'm kinda quiet."

Determined to dissolve her discomfort, he took another drink and nodded. "For the next five minutes, forget I'm your boss."

She gave him a doubtful look and shook her head.

"It's an order."

Still doubtful, she sighed. "I'll try."

"You have a cat."

Amanda smiled. "Yes, Delilah. She's been spayed, but the neighbors in my apartment call her a—" she paused, then shrugged "—slut for human attention."

His lips twitched in amusement. "So, you live with a slut?"

"Yes, I've tried to reform her, but it's futile."

"What do you do when you're not working?"

"Well, I have a very demanding and challenging job, so I don't have a lot of time to spare."

"Nice try. Now give the real answer."

"I belong to a fitness club where I swim a few times each week. I volunteer with a professional advocacy organization for teenage girls and I have friends I join for lunch, dinner and shopping. Are you asleep yet?"

"No," he said and swallowed a chuckle. "Men?"

She paused and seemed almost to hold her breath. "Not at the moment."

He nodded, not quite sure why he'd asked that question. "What do you think of your boss?"

She gave him a long-suffering glance, and Jack wondered how he'd missed the stories her eyes could tell. She looked away again. "He is very challenging and demanding, but also rewarding. Intelligent, makes things happen," she said. "He leaps tall buildings in a single bound, but he is occasionally human." Her gaze slid to the brass clock on the mantel and she handed him her still-full wineglass. "Five minutes is up."

"I didn't notice."

"You weren't the one under the microscope," she said with gentle reproof, and stood. "Thank you for the wine. Your daughter is beautiful and sweet. You're lucky. If you ever need me to pinch-hit again, let me know."

He frowned thoughtfully as she turned away. "Amanda," he said, stopping her with his voice.

She turned, her arms wrapped around herself as if she were braced for another trip under the microscope. "Yes?"

He detested asking the question, hated that he didn't have the answer himself. "Why is my daughter afraid of me?"

Her face softened. "You said yourself that she hasn't spent much time with you. You're larger than life to her. So tall, so strong. Even your voice is strong."

"That's why she whispers," he muttered, and took another sip of whiskey.

"She doesn't know your secret yet."

He narrowed his eyes and cocked his head. "And what is my secret?"

"That you would do just about anything to make her happy. When she learns that, you're cooked." She met his gaze with gentle reassurance. "She'll be okay. You'll both be okay."

Jack watched Amanda walk out of the room and wondered how his assistant knew so much more about him than he knew about her.

TWO

He had *looked* at her.

Amanda stared wide-eyed at the ceiling in the guest bedroom of Jack's home. She was wearing his pajamas, sleeping in his house.

All because she was good with kids, her rational mind reminded her. And she was *not* sleeping.

But he had looked at her. She had seen and felt the curiosity in his gaze. Her mind was whirling. When he'd asked her to forget he was her boss, she'd nearly dropped her wineglass. Did this represent some kind of breakthrough? Did this mean she was no longer invisible?

Taking a deep breath, her defense mechanisms kicked in and she closed her eyes. Probably not a breakthrough, she reasoned. Probably an aberration. She felt a clinch of disappointment at the same time she felt relief. Maybe she really wasn't the right woman for Jack Fortune. The man might be a master communicator with clients, but he made her nervous.

Carol had once told her she thought Amanda was comfortable with Jack being her unreachable dream. Amanda had pooh-poohed the idea, but now she wondered if there was a grain of truth to it. It was much easier to be silently and secretly enthralled with Jack than it was to try to carry on a conversation with him that didn't involve work.

She rolled onto her side and sighed into her pillow. He was still the most exciting man she had ever met. Tonight was an aberration. Tomorrow she and Jack would return to the office, and she would become invisible again. Everything would be normal.

The following morning Amanda put on her wrinkled suit, brushed the tangles from her hair and avoided looking into the mirror. She just didn't want to know what she looked like.

She stepped into the kitchen and found Jack talking with a stern-looking, older woman. "Lilly, Mrs. Downey will take care of you today since Ms. Brown is still sick."

Amanda glanced at Lilly and immediately saw the little girl's feelings on the subject. The telltale protrusion of her bottom lip, followed by too-shiny eyes grabbed at Amanda's heart.

Lilly shook her head, and in the middle of one shake, she spotted Amanda and ran to her. In her timid, whispered voice, she asked, "Can you stay with me?"

Amanda ruffled Lilly's hair. "Oh, sweetie, I wish I could, but I work for your daddy at his office and—"

Attaching her small frame to Amanda's leg, Lilly started to sob. Amanda looked helplessly at Jack.

"Excuse me, Mrs. Downey," he said quietly and moved to Amanda's side. "Let's take her to the office."

Amanda stared at him. "Pardon me?"

"The Eastco deal is done. It will be a light day," he said.

"Easy for whom?" Amanda asked, knowing how quickly her work piled up in her absence. "I was gone yesterday. Remember?"

"I remember. It will be a light day," he told her. "I promise. The poor kid's been through too many changes lately. This one isn't necessary."

Amanda felt the intensity of his gaze down to her bones. She hadn't become invisible again. Yet. With Lilly clinging to her and Jack looking at her that way, she had no choice. "Okay," she said.

Jack glanced at Mrs. Downey. "We've had a change of plans, but I'd like to compensate you for coming out on such short notice."

After quickly downing cereal, toast and milk, the three of them piled into Jack's Mercedes and headed for Amanda's town house apartment on the other side of town. Showing no favoritism, Delilah greeted them at the door, swirling between each pair of legs.

Lilly squealed with delight.

Jack quirked his lips into a wry grin. "The slut?" he asked in a voice for Amanda's ears only.

"I didn't exaggerate. Let me get dressed. It will only take a few minutes. Make yourselves at—" She broke off, the comparison between her comfortable but modest apartment and Jack's luxurious home hitting her. "Have a seat," she said instead.

Lilly wandered upstairs and watched Amanda lose a battle with a curling iron. When Amanda applied lipstick, the little girl puckered her lips; a silent invitation for Amanda to paint her tiny mouth, too. Amanda smiled and complied, then put on her pearl earrings. Digging through the jewelry box, Lilly selected the gaudy rhinestone drop earrings Amanda had received as a gag gift and never worn.

Chuckling, she clipped the large earrings on Lilly's little ears. "Oh, your daddy is going to love these. Let's go."

They walked downstairs, and Amanda watched Jack do a double take at his daughter. "She has excellent taste, wouldn't you say?" Amanda asked.

Audibly swallowing his amusement, he nodded. "You look beautiful, Lilly."

"This is when you say thank you," Amanda whispered to Lilly.

"Thank you," Lilly echoed in a whisper.

Lilly was a hit at the office until just after lunch, when the little girl's energy began to wane, boredom began to set in and naptime loomed. After much coaxing, coddling and a promise of cookie and juice after the nap, Amanda was able to persuade Lilly to lie down on a sofa in an office down the hall.

Amanda plopped down in her chair, cradled her

chin in her hands and closed her eyes. A nap sounded pretty good to her right now, too.

"Sleeping on the job?" Jack asked in an amused voice.

Chagrined, she immediately straightened.

He leaned against her desk. "How did you get her to take a nap?"

"Complex negotiations. It would require too much of your time to explain."

"You pulled the cookie trick again, didn't you?"

"Think about it. If a nap followed by juice and cookies were part of the required schedule for the United Nations, I bet our conflicts would significantly decrease."

He nodded. "Point taken. I need you in my office. I've got a new project in mind for you."

Amanda's silly heart leaped at his words. *I need you.*

"Okay," she managed, and pulled herself back in line. "Now?"

"Yes," he said and led the way.

Following him, she waited expectantly after he closed the door. Gazing at her thoughtfully, he remained quiet for far too long.

Amanda's stomach began to dance with uneasiness.

He slowly walked toward her and stopped. "I need you..." he began, sending her heart into another tripping mode. She wished he would stop that.

"...to move in with me and take care of Lilly for a while."

Move in with me. Amanda locked her knees. Her head began to swim. *Move in with me.* His words echoed in her mind. She didn't even think she'd fantasized hearing those before.

"I know it's an unusual request, but Lilly needs you. I need you to help her during this time of transition for her. She never really liked Ms. Brown that much, but she adores you."

Amanda slammed the brakes on her thoughts. This was all about Lilly. This was not about Jack or his feelings for Amanda. The knowledge rubbed at a raw spot inside her. She took a mind-clearing breath. "But didn't you tell me the doctor said Ms. Brown should get over her flu in a few days? And she'll be able to take care of Lilly again?"

"Yes and no. She'll recover, but I called her today and asked her honestly how she felt her position was working out with Lilly. Ms. Brown said Lilly still didn't seem happy, and she wondered if another personality might suit better."

Amanda felt a sinking sensation in her stomach. "You didn't let her go."

"I did."

Amanda shook her head. "Oh, Jack. I'm not a nanny. I'm an administrative assistant."

"But you're great with Lilly."

"What about my job?"

"I've arranged for a replacement," he told her.

Amanda felt as if she'd been kicked. "That easily?"

"No!" he said, raising his voice. "Dammit, not that easily." He raked a hand through his hair. "My little girl has been miserable since she came to live at my house. I can't help her. The nanny can't help her. But you did. What choice do I have?''

"You were sure I would agree, weren't you?''

"I hoped. It's not forever. It's just until she adjusts to living with me. Afterward, you'll have your job back," he said. "And my undying gratitude."

Amanda sighed and walked away from him. She felt torn. If she stayed at Jack's house, she would be in intimate contact with him on a daily basis. It wouldn't be all business between them. She could end up falling more deeply for him. She could, in fact, fall irrevocably for him. It was a terrible risk to take.

She glanced at him, and the combination of ruthless determination and vulnerability stamped on his face quashed her inner protests.

Carol would either tell her she was crazy or that this was an opportunity she couldn't pass up. This could be Amanda's only chance with Jack. This could be her chance to stop being the invisible woman. Maybe Jack would really see her, and maybe if he saw her, he would also see that she was meant for him.

"I still need to keep up my activities and classes. I will want to keep up with my friends."

"Consider it done."

"My cat will have to move in."

He paused a millisecond. "Okay."

"I will want to oversee the person temporarily assigned to this position, so I don't come back to a mess."

"Makes sense."

She rolled her eyes. "I've never seen you this

agreeable. Should I ask for a million in unmarked bills?''

He chuckled. "You might be surprised. You'll do it?"

"I need to know that you'll be spending time with Lilly in the evening and on the weekends."

"I will. I would have before, but you know that Sandra made it difficult," he said, meeting her gaze. "Anything else?"

"Just one thing," Amanda said.

"Here comes the million in unmarked bills," he said cynically.

"Not quite," Amanda said, surprised at the slight edge of bitterness in his tone. She'd never heard it directed toward her before. "Once a week I'll bring Lilly to your office and you will have lunch with her."

Jack looked at her as if she were an alien he could never hope to understand. "I was certain you'd ask for more compensation," he muttered. "Is that all?"

"Yep. I'm warning you, though. If your goal is Lilly in starched pinafores and speaking when spoken to, you've just gotten yourself into a doozy of a mess."

His expression turned thoughtful, and she saw a rare glimmer of vulnerability in his strong features. "My goal is to make Lilly happy."

Her heart caught. "I'll do my best."

The following week Jack took an overseas trip for the purpose of cultivating an international account. Although his days were filled with meetings and business lunches and dinners, his mind frequently wandered to thoughts of Amanda and Lilly. He placed a couple of transcontinental calls home and was relieved to hear all was well.

His meetings went so well he arrived home one day early. Jack entered his foyer to the sounds of laughter and the "Limbo" song. Delilah greeted him by weaving between his legs and purring. Following the sound of the music, he walked into the kitchen and saw his daughter and Amanda doing the limbo underneath a jump rope stretched across two kitchen chairs.

Amanda, barefoot and dressed in jeans and a cropped shirt, shimmied under the rope, her movements baring her belly to his gaze. "I don't know about this, Lilly," she said. "I'm not sure I can—"

Distracted by the curve of her waist, he watched her stumble. Hearing her little squeak, he automatically grabbed her to keep her from falling. Amanda stared at him.

Her hand clung to his, and he secured her with his other hand on her back. No bra, he idly noticed. His staid, conservative secretary wasn't wearing a bra. A strange sizzling sensation spread through him. Her mouth formed an O of surprise. She had a pretty, lush mouth, he thought. He hadn't noticed it before.

"You're home early," she finally managed, still holding his hand.

"I wrapped things up quickly." He pulled her to her feet.

Her eyelashes fluttered, and her cheeks turned pink. She looked down at their joined hands. "Oh," she said, and removed her palm from his as if it had been burned.

Jack would have sworn he'd seen her fingers tremble slightly when she'd lifted her hand to her forehead, but that couldn't be true. And he sure as hell wasn't feeling a kick of arousal.

Amanda made a sound resembling a faint chuckle, then, seeming to gather her composure, she turned to Lilly. "It must be your day, sweetie. You beat me at limbo, and your daddy's here!" She cut off Lilly's tape player and put her arm around his daughter. "He has been cooped up in an airplane for a long time, and I bet he rushed back just so he could see you. I bet he also needs a hug."

Hesitating, Lilly eyed him with a mixture of wariness and childlike sympathy. With slow steps she moved toward him, and when he bent down, she wrapped her arms around his neck.

Jack's heart dipped. He picked her up and squeezed her small frame to him. "Hi, princess. Have you had a good time with Amanda?"

Lilly nodded.

"Have you been a good girl?"

Lilly nodded.

"Very good," Amanda added. "Plus she was smearing me during the limbo dance. Since it was going to be just us girls tonight, Lilly asked if we could have spaghetti instead of the chicken cordon bleu the housekeeper left. I can heat up the chicken for you if you like?"

Jack shook his head. "Spaghetti's fine." He set

Lilly down when she began to squirm. "I'll clean up and be back down."

After dinner and kissing Lilly good-night, Jack poured a drink in the den. Hearing the soft click of a door closing, he glanced out the window and saw Amanda on the back porch. He picked up a newspaper and skimmed it for a few minutes, then checked the window again. She still sat on the porch. He strolled outside.

"Nice night," he said.

"Almost every night," she said, rolling her shoulders. "I found out there's less glare from the city lights here, so the evening sky looks beautiful."

"I hadn't really noticed," he murmured.

"You've been busy making conquests," she said, looking at him.

"Conquests?"

"Corporate conquests. How many international companies did Fortune's Marco Polo conquer this time?"

He quirked his mouth at her reference to his reputation. "Lots of interest. One commitment."

"Good for you," she said with a smile, then rubbed her left shoulder.

"Got a problem, there?" he asked.

"Just a little tight. I think I did one too many rounds of the limbo," she admitted.

"Where is it?"

"Right here," she pointed. "But—"

Jack put his hands on her shoulder and felt the small knot. He rubbed and massaged her shoulders while Amanda fell silent. She let out a quiet moan that pulled at his gut. Her cropped shirt was thin, and he remembered she wasn't wearing a bra.

Brushing aside the thought, he continued the massage. "You're very quiet."

"You haven't ever rubbed my shoulders before," she said.

"Is it helping?"

"You—" she took a careful breath "—you're very good."

Her words were both an unwitting sensual compliment and invitation, and he wondered what Amanda was like in bed. Was she conservative and repressed, the way she was in the office? Or uninhibited, like she was with his daughter? How responsive would she be? What would make her sigh and gasp? How would her nipples respond to his fingers and mouth?

He felt the dull ache of arousal between his legs. Over Amanda? Jack shook his head.

"You're different here from the way you are at the office."

"Different jobs," she said slowly as if she were forcing herself to concentrate. "With Lilly, she needs me to act a little crazy to get her to come out of herself. She needs lots of hugs." She made a soft moan.

"And at the office?" he prompted, his curiosity about his assistant growing. There was more about Amanda than met the eye.

"At the office you need me to be efficient and to anticipate your needs so your time won't be wasted." She sighed and leaned away from him. "Thank you," she said. turning slightly to face him. "You need me to be invisible." A lock of hair slid over one of her eyes like a filmy shield of her secrets. Meeting his gaze, she gave a soft, wry smile. "I'm very good at being invisible."

Amanda said good-night, and Jack stayed awake. Although he was tired, he couldn't sleep because of the time zone change. In the middle of the night while he surfed through late-night television, he thought about Amanda. He decided that perhaps she had a few surprises behind those big brown eyes. Maybe she wasn't just background music after all.

Two days later Amanda brought a picnic lunch for Lilly and Jack to share at the office while she answered questions from her replacement, took care of transition confusion and grabbed a lightning-quick lunch with Carol in a snack bar. "I want an update," Carol demanded.

"Lilly's such a sweetie. She—"

"Jack. I want an update on your progress with Jack, since you have now penetrated the Fortune outer wall."

Amanda laughed and shook her head. "I'm not that much of a schemer. I've been much busier with Lilly than Jack."

Carol frowned. "But part of your purpose in taking on this job was making Jack Fortune see you as a woman."

"Well, I think maybe he does," she said, thinking of the questions he'd asked her and the way he'd looked at her. "There've been a few nights that we talked."

"Talk?" Carol asked. "Talk is *all?*"

"Mostly," Amanda said. "He rubbed my shoulder one night, but—"

"A massage. That's better." Carol studied her. "Your eyes are sparkling."

Amanda felt her cheeks heat, remembering the way his hands had felt on her. She'd barely been able to breathe, let alone think or talk. It had been torture to pull away, but if she'd allowed him to continue, she'd feared she would do something crazy like turn around in his arms and kiss him. Although Amanda was finding it more and more difficult to keep her feelings invisible to Jack, she was determined to keep her hopes under control.

"No. My eyes are not sparkling." She shook her head at both Carol and her crazy hopes. "Nothing has happened. He hasn't professed undying love, nor does he seem to have gotten a big eureka that I'm the woman of his dreams. Nothing has happened," she said again to keep herself on the ground.

"Uh-huh," Carol said in disbelief. "Your eyes are sparkling, and it's not due to new contact lens."

Amanda changed the subject, then scooted back to work a few minutes later. On her way to her office she saw Mollie Shaw hanging outside Stuart Fortune's office.

Amanda knew Mollie was Chloe Fortune's young wedding consultant, but she'd only spoken to her a couple of times. "Can I help you find something?"

Mollie blushed. "Oh, no. I—uh—" She bit her lip.

"I—uh—I was looking for Emmet, Chloe's father. I needed to discuss some of the wedding arrangements with him."

"With Emmet," Amanda repeated doubtfully. "Emmet's office is on the next floor."

"Oh," Mollie said, her cheeks deepening with color. "My sense of direction needs a little work. Thanks," she said, then quickly breezed away.

Puzzled, Amanda looked after her for a long moment. She returned to Jack's office, gave a quick hug to Lilly and an update to Jack.

"Thanks," he said. "Your replacement is having a difficult time."

"Why?"

"Because I start every sentence with 'Amanda does it this way.'"

She smiled. "Are you saying you miss your invisible assistant?"

A curious, seductive light flickered in his green eyes. "You might have been invisible, but what you did wasn't," he told her. "I have a conference in fifteen minutes. Is there anything else?"

"Not really," Amanda said, thinking of Mollie Shaw. "Except I just saw Mollie Shaw hanging around Stuart's office. She said she was here to see Emmet, but she seemed very nervous." She shrugged. "It's probably nothing. Will you be home for dinner tonight?"

"No. I'm joining Trina. Time for that rain check."

Amanda felt her stomach sink and instantly chided herself. Just because she was caring for Jack's daughter and the nature of the conversations had become more personal didn't mean he was anywhere near having romantic feelings for her. Just because he'd seemed to look at her, really look at her, a few times, didn't mean he wanted anything from her except to help Lilly be happy.

She made herself smile. "Have a good time," she said, feeling the sparkle inside her fizzle.

Three

————

Mason Chandler stopped Jack outside the conference room after his afternoon meeting. "Got a minute?"

"Sure. My office?"

Mason nodded, and they walked down the hall. A successful businessman in his own right, Mason had long moved in the same social circle as the Fortune family. Soon he would be joining their ranks as Jack's cousin Chloe's husband. Even though he owned his own company, he was well trusted by the Fortune family.

"Hold my calls, Elaine," Jack said to his replacement assistant, then joined Mason in his office. "What's up?"

"Chloe told me your father's been acting edgy lately," Mason said.

Jack frowned.

"Will you keep me posted if you see or hear anything out of the ordinary? Anything at all."

Jack shrugged. "I can't think of anything off-hand," he said. "Unless— It's nothing."

"You'd be surprised what can come from nothing," Mason said in a dark tone.

"Amanda told me Mollie Shaw was hanging around Stuart's office. When Amanda asked her about it, she got nervous. It's probably nothing," he said. "Mollie's barely over drinking age."

"Maybe a background check," Mason murmured.

"For a wedding planner?" Jack asked in disbelief. "Are we stepping into paranoia? Besides, she's good friends with your future brother-in-law's wife, Kelly."

"You may be right," Mason said in a noncommittal voice. "But there is such a thing as healthy paranoia. Keep your eyes open. Okay?"

"Always," Jack said. "How do you get all your information, anyway?"

"I have my sources." Mason headed for the door and turned around. "How's Lilly?"

"Better since Amanda took over."

"That's good. You headed home now?"

"No, I'm meeting Trina Sullivan for dinner."

"Redhead." Mason cracked a wicked grin. "Jack's new WOW."

"'Wow'?" Jack repeated.

"Woman of the week. You don't keep them around much longer than that."

"I come from a long line of matchmakers," Jack told Mason. "You know about Kate," he said referring to his aunt who was determined to make sure all

Fortunes were happily married and producing more heirs. "The only way to throw her off course is to be a moving target."

"No serious contenders?"

"The only female I'm serious about is Lilly."

Mason nodded slowly. "Safe choice. 'Night."

After Mason left, Jack checked the mirror in his office rest room and straightened his tie. His evenings had been too quiet lately. He'd had too much time to reflect. He needed a distraction. Trina.

Every time Amanda closed her eyes that night in bed, she pictured Jack. And Trina. He would flirt with Trina and let his hand linger at her waist. He would kiss her. He would hold her.

Pain cut through her. Jealousy welled inside her. Amanda squished her eyes closed. She hated jealousy. It was such a small, useless emotion. Amanda didn't spend much time lamenting her plain appearance. Her value had never been in the color of her eyes, the shape of her face or the shape of her slim body. She'd been valued for her mind, her common sense and for her heart.

Her mother had always said outer beauty faded, but inner beauty lasted forever. Amanda knew those qualities were important for the long run. When she thought of Jack and Trina, however, she wished for just a little more outer beauty.

She heard the front door close, and her eyes popped open. Jack was home. Her heart pounded against her rib cage. She glanced at the clock. Past midnight. Would he smell like her perfume? Would her lipstick be on his mouth and his neck? Had she teased his mind? Worse yet, she wondered, her stomach twisting, had Trina touched his heart?

Amanda had no idea how she would get through this weekend. She would have to avoid Jack as much as possible.

Late Sunday night, Amanda heard Lilly cry out. The heartrending sound jerked her awake faster than an ice-cold shower. Lilly cried out again, and Amanda tossed back her covers and rushed down the hall to the little girl's room.

Nightmare. Amanda watched Lilly toss and turn with her eyes still closed. She gently awakened her. "You're dreaming, Lilly."

"Mommy—" Lilly's eyes blinked open and she began to sob. "I want my mommy."

Her heart twisting at the well of grief and confusion in Lilly's voice, Amanda took her into her arms. "Oh, sweetie. I'm so sorry."

"I—want—" Lilly sniffed and sobbed. "I—want her to come back."

"I know you do," Amanda said, holding Lilly tight. She remembered her own bottomless sadness when her father had died.

"She's not coming back, is she?"

It hurt Amanda to see Lilly in such pain, to have to be the one to kill her futile wish. "She's not. She can't. I'm sure she would if she could. She may not be with you the way she used to be, but you can keep her alive in your mind and heart forever." She flicked on the bedside lamp. "Let's look at her picture again."

From the doorway, Jack watched in wonder as

Amanda comforted Lilly. It was as if she knew exactly what to do. There was a depth to Amanda he'd clearly never appreciated. She said the things about his former wife he never would have thought to say because of his bitterness toward her.

Amanda's generosity touched a secret place inside him, and he felt something inside him shift. Moved, he drank in the scene. Amanda wore a white cotton nightgown. Her hair tousled, her face stripped of makeup, she shouldn't have been sexy to him. He found himself noticing her bare legs and wanting her softness.

Delilah distracted him by weaving around his legs, then prissing into Lilly's room.

"Look who came to see you," Amanda said. "She can't stand being left out of any girl talk."

"Can she stay?" Lilly asked.

"I don't know if your daddy—"

"Daddy says it's fine," Jack said, moving into the room. "You okay, princess?"

Lilly's brave nod made his chest tighten. He reached down to kiss her and ruffle her hair. "I don't know how I got the very best daughter in the world. I guess I just got lucky."

She slipped her hands around his neck and squeezed him.

"It'll be better in the morning," he told her. "Get some rest."

Amanda turned off the light and followed him out of the room.

"Thank you," he said after she closed the door.

"For what?" she asked.

"For helping her."

"When I heard her cry, I couldn't have done anything else. It was like someone had grabbed my heart and smashed it."

Jack nodded. "Yes, but you knew what to do."

Amanda heard a trace of longing in his tone. "Hugs help a lot."

He sighed. "At the office I never second-guess myself. I know what to do. But with Lilly," he said, shaking his head.

"That will change," Amanda assured him, too aware of his presence in the darkened hallway. She tried not to be aware of his muscular bare chest and thin sleep trousers. "You've been training for Fortune Corporation your entire life. Being a daddy takes a different kind of practice."

He turned to her outside her room. "I didn't see much of you this weekend. Why?"

Amanda's stomach dipped. "I thought it might be best if Lilly had a little more time alone with you, so I made myself scarce," she said, and prayed she wouldn't be struck by lightning for telling a half-truth.

He moved closer, his gaze holding hers intently. "We missed you."

Her heart rate kicked up. Although he'd said *we*, he'd meant Lilly, she told herself. "Lilly has gotten used to me being around. She'll get used to you, too."

"I've gotten used to you being around," he muttered as if he weren't entirely pleased. He lifted his hand to her jaw. "You're more than I thought you were."

Amanda could barely breathe, let alone say a word.

"How did you hide it from me?"

She took a shallow breath and inhaled his masculine scent. "I was supposed to be invisible," she whispered. "That's what you needed from me."

"You know more about me than I know about you. Not fair." He narrowed his green eyes slightly. "Are you sure you didn't fool me into believing you were invisible?"

"I did not fool you," she said, full voice. "You were too busy wor—" She broke off, unwilling to go there. "You just didn't see me."

He wove his finger through a strand of her hair. "I was too busy doing what?"

Amanda truly didn't want to discuss this. In fact, she wouldn't mind being invisible again for the rest of this conversation. She closed her eyes. "You were too busy being perfect at work and recovering from your—"

"Failure," he said in a harsh voice.

"Disappointments," she corrected and opened her eyes. "Everyone has disappointments."

His nostrils flared as he took in a sharp breath. She could tell he didn't totally accept her version.

His scent and nearness made her bold. "You're the kind of man who likes to believe that if you try hard enough you can make anything happen."

"I can," he said with confidence, not arrogance.

"But you can't always control everyone else's actions."

"You know too much about me, and I don't know near enough about you," he told her, then lowered his head.

His mouth took hers, and her heart stopped. Unable to close her eyes, her vision blurred. She almost couldn't believe he was kissing her. His lips were supple and persuasive like his voice.

It took a full moment of him brushing his mouth back and forth against hers before she could unlock. Amanda let out the breath she'd been holding, and Jack deepened the kiss. He leaned closer so that his hard chest skimmed her breasts.

He gently, seductively squeezed her jaw, coaxing her to open her mouth as he explored her with his tongue. Amanda felt as if he were teasing her secret emotions from her. She was dizzy from the scent and taste of him.

Here was the man she had been in love with for four years, and he was kissing her like he wanted her. The knowledge made her light-headed. She slid her arms to his shoulders to steady herself, and he stepped between her legs, all the while leading her in a dance of pleasure with his mouth.

He slipped his hand down her throat inside the loose collar of her cotton nightgown. Amanda didn't think to stop him when he cupped her breast. She had ached for his touch so long. She couldn't believe how right it felt to be in his arms.

His thumb played over the turgid tip of her nipple, and desire, swift and shockingly intense, rushed through her. She strained against him.

Jack groaned in approval and slid his other hand down to press her hips against his. Hard with desire, he rubbed against her. He made her feel sexy. She wanted his bare chest against hers. She wanted more.

His hand traveled beneath her gown, and when he found her naked bottom, he groaned again. He cupped her, then moved his hands between her legs. Her breath hitched when he touched her intimately.

She sucked his tongue deeply into her mouth. He thrust his finger inside her and she jerked.

"So warm, tight, soft," he muttered, moving her hand to his hard shaft.

The contrast of his silk trousers against his full hardness turned her to liquid. She caressed him while he devoured her mouth. He wanted her. She could feel it in his kiss, in the way he held her. He made her want to give him everything. She couldn't fathom holding anything back from him.

"Oh, Amanda…" He took her mouth again, then pulled back and swore under his breath.

He stared at her with an expression of sexy disbelief. He rubbed his thumb over her tender lips and eased away from her. Shaking his head, he rubbed his hand over his face. "I don't know what to say. You've surprised me. I didn't expect—"

"Neither did I," she quickly said, unsure whether or not he was pleased with the surprise. Not meeting his gaze, she glanced down. She wasn't sure she wanted him to see how aroused she still was. "It's okay," she added.

She heard him sigh. "Okay," he said, and briefly squeezed her arm. "You better get some sleep. Lilly will be up early."

Amanda nodded and blindly turned toward her doorway. Jack's voice stopped her.

"Are you sure you're okay?"

"Of course," she managed to say, walking into her room. "Good night."

As soon as she closed her door behind her, she

exhaled and slumped against it. Her head was spinning, her body was hot. Stiffening her shaky knees, she crossed the room to push open her window and drink in the cool night air. She saw a hundred stars and knew she'd made a wish on each of them that someday Jack Fortune would notice her—that someday Jack Fortune would want her—that someday Jack Fortune might love her.

Amanda's chest swelled with hope. She closed her eyes and hugged herself. Could it be true? she wondered. Was this the beginning? At long, long last, would her wishes finally come true?

Early the following morning, Amanda opened her door to a quiet knock. "I'd like to talk with you in the study before I leave," Jack said. "Five minutes?"

She blinked the sleep from her eyes. He sounded urgent. "Sure. I just need to get dressed."

Hurriedly putting on shorts and a tank top, then throwing cold water on her face, rinsing her mouth with mouthwash, then brushing her hair, she met him in the study.

Dressed in his suit, he stood facing the window, his profile serious. She felt a sliver of apprehension. "Is something wrong?"

He inhaled quickly and turned to face her. "Yes," he said crisply. "I need to apologize for my behavior last night."

"Oh, no," she said, shaking her head. "You didn't do—"

"I took advantage of your presence in my home."

"Not really," Amanda said.

He cocked his head to one side. "How not really?"

She gulped, feeling her cheeks heat. "Well, in that situation last night, yes, you kissed me, but," she said, lifting her hands, "I kissed you back. So it was two people kissing." *And much more,* she silently added. "I didn't try to stop you," she blurted out.

"Perhaps you should have," Jack said.

Amanda took his words like a jab in the stomach.

"You're the best assistant I've ever had. We have a business relationship, and I'm not going to jeopardize it for some moment of temporary insanity."

Temporary insanity. Amanda felt her newfound hope shatter like glass.

"It was wrong. It shouldn't have happened," he said, his face grim. "I assure you it won't happen again."

If she'd had no pride, she would have asked him if kissing her had been such a terrible experience. Feeling cut up on the inside, she lifted her chin. "You're right. It won't happen again."

Jack nodded. "Good. I'm glad we got that settled. I'm going into the office early today, and I'll probably be late coming home. Don't wait supper for me." He extended his hand to her.

Amanda remembered, just last night, when he'd used that same hand to caress her. Slowly she took his hand and shook it. "I'll tell Lilly," she said, and released his hand.

She watched him leave the room and heard him close the door to the garage behind him. As soon as she saw his car in the driveway, she burst into tears. She felt embarrassed, humiliated and just plain hurt.

For Pete's sake, he'd *apologized* for kissing her.

Amanda knew she wasn't the sexiest woman in Minneapolis, but had it really been that bad?

It hadn't been for her, a voice inside her whispered. Being in Jack's arms had felt so right.

She closed her eyes at her overwhelming feelings. It had obviously been wrong. It was a dream, just a silly dream, she thought. A hard knot of disappointment formed in her throat.

She'd finally gotten Jack to *see* her. He'd even kissed her. But he didn't want her. Oh, how that hurt. She couldn't do a thing, however, to change the truth.

Time to give up the dream.

The realization cut deep. The pain made her sink down into a chair. Even though he hadn't realized it, she'd cared deeply for Jack for such a long time. Working for him all day and worrying about him in the weeks when she'd feared he'd work himself to death after his marriage fell apart, caring intensely for his happiness, had filled her mind and heart. He was such a strong, amazing man that it had been easy to allow him to occupy her mind.

Time to give up the dream.

Amanda fought it, but she knew it was true. She hadn't felt this empty since her mother's death.

"What a jerk," Carol said, pushing her brown bob behind her ear. "Did you tell him to eat bird dookey and die?"

Amanda stirred her coffee and chuckled despite the pain she still felt. She'd brought Lilly in to visit her father, and the two women were grabbing a lunch at a nearby coffee shop. "I confess that didn't cross my mind."

"Well, you're going to quit, aren't you?"

Amanda's stomach clenched. "I considered it for about a minute, but I couldn't leave Lilly right now. She's too fragile. She's been through too many changes."

"It's going to be hard to be around Jack all the time, especially now."

"Maybe," she conceded, "but it wouldn't be right for me to leave." She took a sip of her coffee. "I'm going to make some changes, though. I've been thinking about it for the past few days since Monday's conversation. It's time."

Carol perked up. "A makeover? That would be fun. I know this terrific salon that—"

Amanda held up her hand. "I'm working from the inside out. I might try a new class. I'm going to read some different books." She took a fortifying breath. "I might even go out."

Carol slanted her eyes speculatively. "Sounds like you're reinventing Amanda. That could include Feminine Wiles 101?"

Amanda gave a wry smile. "Only if it's the remedial class."

Over the next week, every time Amanda saw Jack, she hurt, so she made it her goal to avoid him. She started skipping dinner and leaving the house as soon as Jack arrived home. She found that if she timed it just right, she could escape while he was changing his clothes. She returned to put Lilly to bed, then quickly breezed past Jack as he gave his daughter a good-night kiss.

After a week of successful evasions, however, Jack

caught her as she left her bedroom. She told her heart not to beat faster.

"I haven't seen much of you," he said, studying her, his hands on his hips.

"Busy week," she said, trying not to feel.

"This doesn't have anything to do with that night in the hall, does it?"

When you kissed me senseless? When you made me want you so much I was dizzy with it? When I started to believe dreams can come true?

She bit her lip. "No."

Jack cocked his head to one side as if he wasn't convinced. "Are you sure? I told you—"

Unable to bear a replay, Amanda held up her hand. "I know you told me it was temporary insanity for you to kiss me. I understand that you don't want me and will never want me. You're not attracted to me sexually, emotionally or physically. My only value to you is what I do for your daughter and what I do for you professionally. I understand perfectly."

Four

Jack could still feel the breeze as Amanda swept past him, telling him she was meeting friends and wishing him a nice evening.

He was still unsettled by that evening when he'd lost control with her. He couldn't remember experiencing such a rare combination of feelings; arousal, curiosity and a need for her tenderness. Ridiculous, he thought in disgust, tossing the *Investor's Business Daily* on the cherry end-table and standing. He didn't need tenderness. The only things he wanted from a woman were distraction and occasional sexual ease.

Amanda's parting words stuck in his craw. He'd put on an instrumental CD, background music, but it failed to soothe him. It was stupid, he thought, that her opinion and feelings affected him. She was his assistant and the temporary nanny for his daughter.

There was nothing personal between them. Even if he were drawn to her, it wouldn't work out. She was background music.

So why had he missed her during the past week?

Jack scowled and turned off the stereo. Silence immediately enveloped him. He glanced at his watch. Where was she, anyway? She'd never stayed out this late before.

He heard a sound at the front door, the click of a key, stumbling footsteps, a whispered oath. He walked to the foyer and spotted Amanda. Her hair was slightly disheveled, her balance unsteady, her eyes hazy.

It surprised the hell out of him, but he couldn't deny the woman was tipsy. "Problems?"

She jumped and gaped at him. "Oops," she whispered. "Sorry. I had a little problem with the door."

She stumbled and had a *little problem with the wall, too.*

"Need some help?" Jack extended his hand.

Amanda shook her head, then winced. "No, no, no. I'll be fine. I'll just go slow."

Watching her as she carefully put one foot in front of the other, he walked beside her. "Did you drive home?"

She blew a strand of hair from her forehead. "No. Carol brought me home."

"Where did you go?"

"A bar."

"How much did you have to drink?"

"Carol wanted me to taste all the mixed drinks I'd never tried before. I took a sip or two from each one, but there were just too many," she said, shaking her head and wincing again.

Jack felt a flash of anger directed toward Carol. "She doesn't sound like much of a friend."

"Oh, she is," Amanda protested, bumping into the wall again. "She was trying to distract me."

Unable to watch her weaving gait any longer, he steadied her with his hand. "From what?"

"What?" She pushed open the door to her bedroom and allowed him to help her inside.

"Carol tried to distract you from what?"

She lifted her dark gaze to his. "From you," she whispered.

She was tipsy and dizzy, speaking out of turn, and she shouldn't have seemed sexy to him. But she did. He suspected he could get more than a few grains of truth from Amanda right now, and he was curious and bothered enough to take advantage of the situation. "Why me?"

"Because you," she said, pointing her finger at his chest, "are my big *oh-no.*"

This was going to take some work, he thought. He needed an interpretation. "Your big *oh-no,*" he repeated.

She nodded and sighed.

"Why am I your big *oh-no?*"

"Because I did something really stupid. I worked for you. I watched you win, and I watched you lose. I watched you get hurt, and I did something really stupid." She shook her head sadly.

"What did you do?"

"I fell in love with you."

She might as well have punched him. He stared at

her face in the moonlight from her window, and though he saw the flush of alcohol, there was stark honesty in her eyes.

"Big *oh-no*," she muttered and sighed. "But you don't have to worry because I'm going to stop loving you. I even bought a book."

"A book," he echoed, feeling the most peculiar sense of loss. She sounded determined.

"Yeah, it's called *How To Fall out of Love*. I'm dizzy," she said, and sank down on the edge of the bed. She dropped her head into her hands. "I never realized there were so many different kinds of mixed drinks."

"Are you going to be sick?"

She shook her head and winced. "No. I just need to lie down," she said, and slowly fell back on the bed.

Her hair splayed out silky and soft on either side of her flushed face. Her lips were parted, her eyes hooded in mystery. He remembered how her mouth had tasted beneath his, how her nipples had hardened against his chest, how she had grown liquid and eager for him so quickly. He remembered wanting to slide inside her. At this moment she looked ready for love, Jack thought, and again felt a forbidden need to take her. He squelched it.

"Do you want to change your clothes?"

"After the room stops moving," she said, and closed her eyes.

Jack watched her for a few moments. He didn't know who would regret this conversation more, Amanda or him. He left the room, again stuck with the surprising taste of loss.

* * *

Amanda awakened next morning to the mother of all headaches. Her head throbbed as if someone was banging her with a sledgehammer. The sliver of sunlight through her curtain hurt her eyes, her mouth felt like cotton, and the sound of Lilly's knock on her door might as well have been a gong.

Carefully easing herself into a sitting position, she clutched her head. "Just a second, sweetie," she called, and her own voice vibrated through her head.

She shuddered, but pulled herself to her feet and opened the door. Lilly stood with Jack beside her. Barefoot, with damp hair, he wore a pair of jeans and a T-shirt that emphasized the muscles in his arms and chest. He also wore a slightly mocking grin.

"I told her I thought you might not feel well this morning, but I couldn't persuade her to wait any later," Jack said.

"Hi, sweetie," Amanda said, giving Lilly a hug.

"Are you sick?" Lilly whispered, concern darkening her green eyes.

Amanda shook her head and winced. "Not sick. I just don't feel great this morning. I'll feel better later," she said. "Would you like to feed Delilah all by yourself this morning?"

Lilly nodded hugely, then scampered toward the kitchen.

Amanda felt Jack's gaze and wished she were invisible, truly invisible.

"Have you ever been tipsy before?" he asked.

"No. I always thought it was an incredibly immature and stupid thing to do." She swallowed over her dry throat. "I was right. I may kill Carol," she said, "if I survive. I'll get a shower and some breakfast."

"Take it slow," he cautioned.

"Food or shower?" she asked.

"Both."

She nodded, ready for him to leave, but he stood there still looking at her. "Let me know if you want me to give you a lift to get your car."

"I forgot about that," she said, then fuzzy images from the previous evening slid through her mind. She frowned in concentration. "You helped me to my room last night. Thank you," she murmured, and another image taunted her.

"You're welcome."

A conversation between them echoed through her mind like bricks in a pond. "I, uh—" She cleared her throat. "We, uh, didn't talk much last night, did we?"

"I didn't," Jack said.

Amanda's stomach sank. She covered her eyes. "I didn't say anything about—"

"Falling in love with me?"

Amanda groaned.

"You also told me about the book."

It wasn't possible to be more embarrassed. "People say all kinds of crazy things when they've had too much alcohol."

"It can have an uninhibiting effect."

She sighed. "If you have a kind bone in your body, you'll forget you heard it."

"Not likely," Jack said.

She met his gaze.

"I've never had a woman tell me she loved me in

one breath and in the next assure me that she'll get over me."

Her heart picked up at the masculine challenge in his eyes. Was she imagining it? Confused, she shrugged. "It's nice to know I'll be unique."

He nodded, his gaze seeming to take her apart like a puzzle he was determined to understand. He gave a maddening half grin. "Will it be that easy for you?" he asked in a deep voice.

Her stomach dipped. Was he flirting with her? No, she thought, he couldn't be. "The book will help."

"Let me know if it works," he said, the glint in his eyes mockingly suggestive.

He was too much for her this morning, too much for her eyes and senses, too much for her poor head. Too much for her poor heart. "I'll send you a memo," she mumbled, closing the door as his laughter rumbled through her like the first tremors of an earthquake.

"Kiyah!"

Jack heard the chorus as soon as he opened the front door after work a few days later. He turned the corner to find the extraordinary sight of Amanda and his daughter in white martial arts outfits standing in fighting position in the middle of the kitchen.

"You decided against ballet," Jack said, referring to the lessons Amanda had mentioned in a note she'd left him. She avoided him like the plague. He suspected that instruction was in her book.

Amanda turned and bowed. Lilly bowed, too, and Jack smiled and bowed in response. "Hi, princess. You want to be a karate kid?"

Lilly nodded solemnly, then reached down to pet Delilah.

"I thought about ballet, but I took Lilly with me to my first few karate lessons, and she copied the instructor, so I thought she'd enjoy it." She moved to his side. "There's a funny thing about karate," she whispered.

"What's that?"

"You can't whisper your *Kiyahs.*"

Jack nodded. He had mixed feelings about his little girl taking martial arts.

"You'd rather see her in a pink tutu and leotard?" Amanda asked.

He remembered how happy Lilly had looked when she'd been playing in the mud and shook his head. "Nah. I just want her happy."

"Me, too," Amanda said. "I didn't plan it this way, but she's so shy. I imagine she doesn't feel like she has much control over her life since her mother died. I hate the idea of her feeling like a victim. So maybe a little screaming, kicking and punching would be a good thing."

Jack met Amanda's gaze again and felt a stab of admiration. "How did you get your insight?"

"Experience and observation. Remember, I lost my dad when I was young. And I watch a lot," she said, her gaze darkening.

"You have the advantage," he said, thinking of the years she'd watched him and he'd barely noticed her.

"Advantage over Jack Fortune," she said in disbelief. "How is that?"

"I told you before, you seem to know more about

me than I know about you," he told her. "But that can change. I'm a fast learner."

He saw the sensual light come and go in her eyes. She drew back, and he immediately sensed the distance.

"No need for change," she said. "It's just business as usual between us."

Jack clenched his jaw in irritation. She was merely repeating his words, his wishes. His attitude toward Amanda, however, had been anything but business as usual lately. The more he was around her, the more he wanted to know, and she wasn't making it easy for him.

Amanda continued to avoid Jack over the next few days. It wasn't a matter of convenience. It was a matter of survival. Tonight she'd slipped out the back door to take advantage of the indoor pool while Jack read the paper.

Falling out of love with him was turning out to be more difficult than she'd hoped. If only he weren't so concerned for his daughter. But she wouldn't want that any other way, she told herself, as she swam her third lap on her back. Lilly needed him, and in a special way, Jack needed Lilly. If he weren't kind to his household staff, if he didn't have a sense of humor, if he were uglier...

Amanda sighed and turned over on her stomach, putting her face in the water. Determined to keep her mind focused even though her heart went its own way, she tried one of the techniques from the book. She was so focused she swam straight into Jack.

Her hand encountered bare flesh and she gasped,

sucking in a mouthful of water that went down the wrong way. She hacked and coughed at the tickle in her throat.

Jack patted her on the back, but that only made it worse. She turned away from him and coughed again. At last, she drew a breath, but she still didn't face him. The sight of his muscular bare chest conjured images of the night she wanted to forget. Her blood burned with the memory.

"You surprised me," she finally said and headed for the ladder. "I thought I had the pool to myself."

She felt Jack's hand on her shoulder. "You don't have to go," he said.

She bit her lip. "Oh, it's okay. I just thought I'd swim a few laps to help me sleep."

"Restless at night lately?" he asked.

Amanda took a careful shallow breath. "A little."

"You've been avoiding me."

She didn't bother to deny it. "Yes, I have."

"You haven't sent me a memo on how the book is working," he said.

His light tone nettled her. She turned around. "You think this is funny, don't you?"

"You've got to admit the book is a little…"

Amanda's temper sparked. "A little what? The book was written for people who are desperate. People who have fallen down desperately, hopelessly in love and don't know how to pick themselves up." She lifted her chin and met his gaze. "Have you ever been desperate?"

His eyes turned hard. "After my marriage broke up—"

"It hurt," Amanda said. "But were you desperate for Sandra?"

He took a deep breath. "No. By the time she left, I was ready for her to go."

"Then you don't know what desperate is, so don't make fun."

"Amanda, we're living in the same house. It's ridiculous for you to avoid me."

"Perhaps, but it's necessary."

"It's crazy."

She sighed. "I don't expect you to understand. *You* have the edge, here. You're not attracted to me, so—"

"I never said I wasn't attracted to you."

Amanda felt his gaze travel over her lips, her throat, then her breasts. Her heart leaped and her mouth went dry. She shook her head. She could accept his laughter far more easily. "Don't be kind. I was wrong. Make fun of the book. It'll be easier for me to—"

"I miss you," he said, as if he weren't pleased about that fact, but accepted it.

Amanda's chest squeezed tight and her eyes burned. "Stop being kind," she said, hating the tremble in her voice.

"I'm not," he said, moving closer to her. "I miss you."

His chest was too bare and muscular, his voice too gently seductive. He was too close, too sexy and too focused on her. And she still wanted him far too much. She gave a breathless wry laugh. "You'll get over it," she said and left the pool.

*   *   *

Jack stifled a groan after he hung up from a brief conversation with his father. It had been a rough day and it wasn't over yet. Stuart had called to arrange a meeting with Jack and his brother. Garrett, a rancher at heart, was in town making one of his rare appearances as legal consultant to Fortune Corporation.

"What's up?" he asked, entering Jack's office.

Jack shook his head. "I don't know. Dad hasn't been acting right. He's worried someone is investigating him."

Garrett poured himself a drink and sat down. "I hadn't noticed."

Jack gave a half grin. "You've been overwhelmed with matrimonial bliss."

Garrett smiled. "Life could be worse than marrying a woman who makes the sun shine. When are you going to belly up to the wedding bar again?"

"No time soon. It's gotta be the right woman this time."

"Sometimes what you want is right in front of your face," Garrett said.

Jack's mind drifted to Amanda, and he immediately dismissed the thought. She was part of the reason for his rough day. Although his new assistant was competent, she didn't anticipate his needs the way Amanda had. He'd never realized how easy she'd made his professional day. She knew his schedule like the back of her hand, understood his method of operation and did a thousand little things that made him comfortable. And damn if he didn't miss her.

He frowned.

"Who is she?" Garrett asked. "Takes a woman to inspire that kind of disgust."

"Nobody."

"Yeah, right," Garrett said in disbelief.

"It's no—"

The door whooshed open, and Stuart strode in. His father had always been the picture of confidence, and someone unfamiliar with him wouldn't have had a clue that Stuart was clearly on edge. Although his father was an imposing figure, Jack saw the little signs, the narrowed eyes, slightly clenched fist and the tension in his walk.

"Hey, Dad," Jack said.

"Dad," Garrett said with a nod.

Stuart nodded shortly and went to the bar. Pouring himself three fingers of whiskey, he swallowed the drink and faced his sons.

He sighed. "There's no easy way to tell you this. I had hoped you would never need to know, but you've got to hear it from me."

Jack felt an ominous dragging sensation in his gut. "Are you sick?"

Stuart shook his head.

"Mom?" Garret asked.

"No. It's nothing like that. It's about something that happened twenty-two years ago. Something I'm ashamed of."

"Twenty-two years," Garrett said.

Stuart looked out the huge window, then seemed to brace himself as he turned back around. "Your mother and I had marital problems. The company was demanding all of my time, and I thought she should understand why I had to be gone so much. I admit I took her for granted. I was foolish. I got my priorities all mixed-up. I lost sight of what was truly important."

"You were separated," Jack said, remembering how confused he'd been when his father had left.

Stuart nodded. "Yes, for a few months."

"Mom always told us everything would be okay," Jack said.

"And it was. But I made a mistake, a big mistake before your mother and I reconciled. I could have lost the best thing that ever happened to me." He blinked as if he felt a sharp pain. "I had an affair. Your mother doesn't know, but I am very concerned that someone knows I made a payment to the woman I was involved with. Her name was Karen Simmons. I think I could be blackmailed."

His father's voice broke. "I can't let Marie find out."

Five

Troubled by his father's news, Jack took the long way home. He remembered when his father had left, so many years ago. He remembered the yelling, the slamming doors and then the silence that lasted until his mother started crying. Their separation had shaken his world.

When his father had returned, it was as if the sun decided to shine again. His mother smiled more, and everything felt right.

Jack remembered how supportive his mother and father had been during his own divorce. After their one rocky period their devotion for each other had never wavered, and he had naively expected his marriage to mirror theirs. But his mother had not married his father for money, and Sandra had clearly married Jack for money.

He wondered how his father had gotten so twisted around that he'd lost sight of what was important. When he'd had a heart, Jack had wondered if he would ever experience the kind of love his parents had shared. He had wondered if he would ever find a woman who loved him for himself, not the Fortune name or money.

An image of Amanda flickered through his mind, and he pushed down on the accelerator. She occupied his mind more and more lately. He found himself just wanting to be in her presence. His first instinct was to deny it, but he stopped himself. Maybe he should find out more about Amanda. Maybe he should find out if she was more than background music.

After all was said and done, Jack saw that what mattered most to his father wasn't money, it was his wife and family. Yet, it had been easy to get side-tracked, blinded. In this way, Jack did not want to follow in his father's footsteps.

His thoughts weighing heavy on his mind, he pulled into his garage and entered his home. Delilah greeted him by curling around his ankles. Knowing she wouldn't stop until he petted her, he reached down and stroked her fur, then walked down the hall.

He opened Lilly's bedroom door and watched her sweet, sleep-flushed face for a long moment. His heart squeezed tight with emotion. This was what mattered to him, he thought. Lilly was what was important to him. He kissed her forehead without making her stir. Quietly, he left her room and closed the door. He stopped outside Amanda's room filled with a dark yearning just to see her.

Giving in to the urge, he stole into her room and

found her asleep, too. She must like having the sun wake her, he thought, because she left the curtains open. Right now the moonlight cast her face in a gentle glow. Her tousled brown hair formed a soft frame for her quietly pleasing face.

When he took the time to look, Jack noticed there was beauty in her simplicity. Her nose was straight, her mouth, small yet lush, her chin just a little stubborn. Her eyelashes were long and curly. He frowned, wondering why he'd never noticed her eyelashes before.

His gaze trailed down her ivory throat to the thrust of her small, firm breasts against her nightgown. Lower still, he knew her waist was slim, her thighs silky, inviting. She would wrap her body around his and give him release. Restless, feeling his body swell with arousal, he glanced back at her face. He wanted to read her mind and find out if she was true, or just another feminine broken promise waiting to happen.

His gaze fell on the bedside table where she'd left a book. Curious, he stepped closer and picked it up. *How To Fall out of Love.* The woman was determined.

He'd told her their relationship was professional. He was reconsidering. Jack thought again of his father and how he'd almost lost what was most important to him.

He picked up the book and quietly carried it out of the room with him.

"Mr. Fortune," his assistant said the following afternoon, "Kate Fortune is on line three." Surprised, he set down his marketing demographic study. The grande dame of his family rarely called him. He wondered what had motivated his great aunt this time. ''Put her through.''

''Jack, dear, this is Kate. Amanda insisted that I needn't call you, but I just want you to know that she is resting comfortably and—''

His chest tightened. ''Amanda!''

''Well, yes. She fell—''

''Fell where?'' he demanded, not getting the information he wanted fast enough.

''At the park. She took Lilly to the park today, and Lilly begged to climb on one of the jungle gyms. She lost her footing and Amanda caught her. Lilly's fine. Unfortunately Amanda lost her footing, too, and hurt her ankle.''

''Is she in the hospital?''

''Oh, no. At home,'' Kate added with a chuckle. ''She called the house and I had just showed up for an impromptu visit with Lilly. My chauffeur, Giles, and I picked Amanda and Lilly up and we all went to the clinic together.'' She paused. ''I thought you would want to know. Lilly just adores Amanda, and I'm sure she must be important to you, too.''

Jack wanted to see Amanda for himself. He checked his watch and schedule, mentally shuffling appointments. ''I have a few things to tie up here, then I'll be home. Thank you, Kate.''

''Not at all. I'm glad to help.''

An hour later Kate greeted him at the door. She was just getting ready to leave. ''Hi, darling,'' she said, tilting her cheek for his kiss. ''You're as gorgeous as ever. I wish I could stay, but Sterling and I have an early dinner planned with Mac and Kelly.''

Jack nodded. He knew his cousin Mac and Kelly's marriage had started out on shaky ground, but everyone could tell they were happy now. Would he ever be so lucky? "Tell them I said hi. And thank you for helping Amanda today."

"Not at all," she said, and paused. "I can't help admiring how well Amanda handles Lilly. If I didn't know better, Amanda loves that child so much she could be her mother. She would be a wonderful mother. A wonderful wife. Something to think about," she mused meaningfully, then gave him an air kiss. "'Bye for now, darling."

Catching the scent of her signature perfume in her wake, Jack felt a wry kick of humor as he headed upstairs. Kate had never been known for her subtlety. She didn't like to plant a seed. She preferred planting an entire garden.

He rounded the corner and found Lilly coming out of the bathroom. Holding her kitty tightly to her, her eyes lit up and she ran to him, bouncing on her toes.

"'Manda's a she-ro. She saved me!"

Jack smiled and crouched down. "She did?"

Lilly nodded emphatically. "I falled off the jungle gym onto 'Manda, and she falled, too." She twisted the stuffed kitty. "I told her I was very sorry, but she said it wasn't my fault. She said she's a klutz."

"Are you hurt?"

Lilly shook her head. "No, but 'Manda yelled when she hurt her leg. She was very brave at the doctor. She didn't cry." She reached for his hand and tugged at him. "She's in her bed."

As they walked to Amanda's room, it occurred to Jack that this was the first time since Sandra's death that Lilly hadn't spoken to him in a whisper. From the doorway, he saw Amanda in bed, with her wrapped ankle propped on pillows and surrounded by Lilly's books.

His heart dipped at the sight, and Kate's words echoed through his head. *She would make a wonderful mother. A wonderful wife.*

"Thank you," he said.

She glanced up, her eyes wide with surprise. "How did you—" She broke off, and realization dawned. "Kate called you. I told her not—"

"I'm glad she did," he said, moving into the room. "I need to know if there's an emergency with you."

Amanda's stomach dipped. Don't be fooled by that look in his eyes, she told herself. He needed to know because she was his daughter's nanny. "I'm sorry you left work. There was really no reason." She found a willing distraction in Lilly. "C'mon sweetie, let me fix your hair."

"How is your ankle?" he asked, standing next to her bed and tugging his tie loose.

Adjusting Lilly's pigtail, Amanda tried not to think about how her heart was racing just because of his presence. "Not too bad. The doctor said I should stay off of it for a day or so." She shook her head and grimaced. "It was just an accident mostly due to my lack of coordination. No karate for me for a while."

"Lilly," Jack said. "I need to talk with Amanda for a few minutes. Can you play in your room?"

Lilly nodded and hugged Amanda before she scampered out of the room with Delilah.

Uneasy, Amanda stacked Lilly's books on top of each other. She didn't want to look at Jack. The damn book wasn't working.

His hand covered hers, and she took a deep breath.

"Thank you for protecting Lilly," he said in a low voice that stroked her heart.

"I couldn't have done anything else," she said, then managed a slight smile. "I just wish I'd been more coordinated."

He skimmed his hand down her leg, setting her nerve endings on fire. "How bad is it really?"

She took another quick breath. "It's, uh—it's not great, but it's not—"

He put his thumb under her chin, coaxing her to meet his gaze. "Really?"

Responding to his demand for the truth, she sighed. "I landed badly."

"Then you need to rest. I'll make arrangements for Lilly," he said.

Hating the idea that she might disrupt Lilly's and Jack's schedules, she shook her head. "I can still keep her with me part of the day. Remember, she takes an afternoon nap and we can read and sing and play—"

"You need to rest that ankle." He ran his fingertips over her toes. "It looks swollen, and I bet you are the kind to push things instead of following the doctor's instructions."

"Doctors are always too cautious," she grumbled.

He chuckled. "You just proved my theory. It's bedtime for you, although if you're going to be in bed for the next few days I can suggest more pleasurable ways to spend it."

Amanda blinked. Had he just flirted with her? She

gave a tiny shake of her head. No. She must have dreamed that last comment.

Jack leaned closer. "You have beautiful eyelashes."

His nearness made her mouth dry.

"It's not mascara, is it?"

She shook her head. "I usually forget to put on mascara."

"Is the book working?" he asked in the same voice he might have used during sex.

It took Amanda a full moment to absorb his question. She drew back immediately. "The book," she echoed.

"How To Fall out of Love," he said, gazing at her as if he not only saw her, but wanted her.

Amanda drew in a quick breath, hoping the delicious scent of his aftershave wouldn't boggle her mind. "I knew you were tough, but I never knew you had a cruel streak," she told him. "You said you wanted a professional relationship with me. You said you didn't want me. I'm doing the best I can to not be in love with you anymore."

He tilted his head, and the predatory look in his eyes made her nervous. "Maybe I don't want you to succeed."

Her heart slammed into her rib cage. "I can't imagine why not."

"I never told you I didn't want you."

"You said kissing me was temporary insanity."

He leaned closer, his mouth a breath from taking hers. "Maybe it wasn't temporary."

A sliver of sanity slid into her brain. *You are in*

over your head. She put her hand against his chest and pushed.

"I don't want to go to maybe land again."

He studied her intently. "I'll have to find a way to persuade you."

His tone was casual, but the determination stamped across his face told Amanda she was in trouble.

Amanda quickly concluded that Jack was playing with her. She had no idea why. Perhaps he was bored. A dangerous state for such a sexually magnetic man. It didn't change the net result for her. She needed to be on her guard. She needed to continue to avoid Jack. She needed to continue falling *out* of love with him. Her task would have been far easier if she hadn't been confined to her bed. Beyond bored, she sneaked out late one night to the pool, unwrapped her ankle and slid into the water.

She did a slow lap on her back, and reveled in a few moments of freedom. The clean water felt like cool satin on her skin, and the buoyancy kept her from hurting her ankle. She stopped mid-stroke when she saw Jack by the side of the pool. He wore jeans and an unbuttoned shirt. His hair was slightly mussed as if he'd raked his fingers through it. Just looking at him made her light-headed.

"I thought everyone had gone to bed," she said.

He shook his head. "Not quite. How were you planning to get back to your room without putting any weight on your ankle?"

"The same way I got out here. Hop," she said.

"And if you fall?"

"Then hopefully I will fall better this time and I

won't wake up the house," she said and ducked her head underwater to keep her head clear.

"That's Plan A?" he asked in a mild tone. "I like Plan B better."

She watched him come closer to the pool. "Plan B? There is no Plan B."

"Yes, there is. Plan B is I carry you to your room so you don't break your pretty little neck."

Panic raced through her. "No. That's really not necessary. I got here under my own steam. I can get back the same way."

"Not in this lifetime," he said with a deadly determined smile.

"This is crazy," she said.

"I agree. It's crazy for you to hop all the way back to your room," he said, crooking his finger at her. "Come here."

"I'm not letting you carry me."

A flicker of surprise darted across his face, then he set his jaw. "Yes, you will."

Amanda stiffened her spine. "I'm staying in here until you leave."

"You're cold," he said, his gaze falling to her breasts. "I can tell."

Amanda felt her nipples taut against her bathing suit and fought embarrassment. "I'm not getting out."

"Okay," he said with a slow nod, then he stepped out of his shoes, pulled off his shirt and undid the top button of his jeans.

Holy moly! Panic shot through Amanda. The man was going to undress right before her very eyes. *Uncle.* "Stop!" she said when she found her breath. Her heart pounding a mile a minute, she pulled herself out of the pool.

His hand lingered near the zipper of his jeans. "You see the wisdom of my suggestion," he concluded.

"It didn't look like a suggestion to me," she told him.

He wrapped her towel around her. "I don't argue about the safety of the people who are important to me." He lifted her into his arms. "Put your arms around my neck."

Amanda hesitated, then reluctantly did as he'd ordered. "I didn't know you were directive in your personal life."

"I don't need to be directive if the person I'm dealing with is reasonable," he said as he carried her through the den to the stairs. "I didn't expect you to be unreasonable."

He made a valid point. It probably wasn't the smartest thing in the world for her to be hopping up and down the stairs. Amanda sighed. "I've been chained to that bed for days."

He carried her into her room. "That image works for me," he said in a silky voice. "You chained to the bed."

Amanda rolled her eyes at his comment and the way her stomach dipped. "Oh, stop. You're just playing with me."

He stopped in the middle of her room and gazed down at her. "Is that what you think?"

"It's what I know," she told him, wiggling to be set down. "I just don't know why."

Jack placed her on the bed, but didn't stand up. His face mere inches from hers, he pushed the towel off her shoulders and ran his finger over the thin shoulder strap of her bathing suit. "What's wrong with playing?"

Her skin felt scored by his touch. "Why are you doing this?" she whispered.

"I want to know you better," he said, sliding his finger to the top of her breast. "Much better." He lowered his finger to her nipple and took her mouth. His tongue slid past her lips, tasting and searching.

Amanda felt herself sinking into the kiss, into him. He tasted dark and forbidden. He felt strong and hot. She felt him pull her strap down and bare her breast to his gaze and his mouth. He suckled her nipple and she felt an insistent tension all the way down her abdomen to her feminine core.

"Your body is so responsive," he said, and curled his tongue around the tip. He gave a rough moan, then slid his lips up her throat to her mouth and kissed her again. As if he sensed she was a mass of desire and confusion, he slowly pulled back from her. "Someday soon, you're going to want me to stay the night," he said. "Someday very soon."

Struggling to clear her head, she lay on the bed in her wet swimsuit and watched him leave. When he closed the door, she covered her face with a hand that trembled. In her dreams, he had kissed her. It had been sweetly passionate. In her dreams, she had envisioned a gentle soft-focused yearning. Her dreams hadn't prepared her for the raw need and breathtaking desire he exhibited and aroused in her. He wasn't quite as tender as she'd imagined. The reality of Jack was more edgy and dangerous. It shook her to the core that Jack's *someday* could have been tonight.

* * *

Over the next few days Jack was attentive yet slightly restrained, as if he was waiting for a signal from her. A signal Amanda wasn't sure she was ready to give. She'd spent years waiting for Jack to notice her. Now he had and wanted an affair. Was that what she truly wanted? Would she fall more deeply, irrevocably in love with him? What would she do once it was over?

What if he was only interested in a physical relationship? That prospect befuddled the daylights out of her. Heaven knows, she wasn't beautiful.

By late Friday afternoon her ankle was better, but she was still in flux about what to do with Jack. Four out of every five moments, she decided she had to take a chance. That last moment, however, was filled with doubt.

After an afternoon walk with Lilly, she fixed the little girl her snack and put her down for a nap. She grabbed a soda from the refrigerator, and the phone rang. "Mrs. Foster, this is Elaine from Mr. Fortune's office."

"Hi, Elaine, this is Amanda. I'm not sure where Mrs. Foster is. Can I take a message?"

"Yes. Remind her that Jack won't be home for dinner tonight."

"Ah, that Sheridan contract causing him problems?"

"No," Elaine said. "He's attending a charity event tonight with Trina. I hear it's a high-dollar event. All of Minneapolis's upper crust is supposed to attend. Rough night, huh?" she said with a laugh.

Amanda felt her heart sink to her toes. "Yeah," she said. "Rough. I'll pass on the message."

She hung up the phone and stared at it. Sick with disappointment, she shook her head at herself. A part of her had started to believe that Jack was interested in her. Jack had fanned the flames to her dying dream, and she had allowed herself to be lulled into believing in crazy possibilities.

Going out with Trina. A sting of anger burned her. Why was he coming on to her at the same time he was dating Trina? Amanda hadn't known that was Jack's approach with women.

Perhaps she had missed some clues along the way. She couldn't imagine getting sexually involved with a man unless it was mutually exclusive. The concept was alien to her. But maybe not to Jack.

She shook her head.

She'd always known she and Jack were from different worlds. If her values were this different from his, then they definitely were not meant to be.

Still staring at the phone, she jumped when it rang. She picked it up and answered it.

"Amanda?" a male voice asked.

"Yes, this is Amanda."

"Jeff Gould, your karate instructor, here. I was wondering how your ankle is healing."

"Almost ready for class," she said, in the mood to kick something at the moment.

"Good," he said. "Next time you have class, would you like to go for coffee?"

No. Her first instinct was to refuse. She'd been refusing dates for over a year. Amanda hesitated. Maybe it was time to start saying yes.

Six

"No, thank you," Amanda said in the matter-of-fact, almost-cool voice Jack had heard all too often lately. He'd invited her to join him and Lilly for their weekly picnic in the office. "I have other plans for lunch."

There was something different about her, Jack thought. Something different in the way she looked at him. Or was it his imagination? It was almost as if she'd looked a little closer at him and hadn't liked what she'd found. The thought gave the same sensation of someone jabbing an elbow in his ribs. He studied her. "How's your ankle?"

"Much better. I'm ready to return to my karate class." She checked her watch. "I'll be back in about an hour. Is that okay?"

Irritated that she was leaving so quickly, he paused. "No," he said to get a reaction from her.

She blinked. "Pardon."

Jack smiled. "Just wanted to make sure I've got your attention." He noticed a stray white hair on the sleeve of her navy jacket and lifted it off. "Delilah left her mark. She's done the same to me a few times."

"I warned you that no human is safe from her feline wiles," Amanda said with a slight smile.

Jack stepped closer to her and touched a strand of her hair. "But you didn't warn me about you."

Amanda's eyes widened, then she gave a husky chuckle. "No need for warning. I don't really have feminine wiles."

"That's a matter of opinion. I like the way you blush when I touch you," he said, stroking her soft cheek with his finger.

Amanda sucked in a quick breath, and her eyes darkened in confusion. "I bet you say that to all the ladies," she said, and looked at Lilly. "Have fun with your daddy. I'll see you in a little bit," she said, and added with a smile, "little bit."

Jack watched her leave, feeling an explicable possessiveness. He wanted inside her head. He wanted inside her. And he would get there.

Amanda grabbed a newspaper in the lobby to keep her company during lunch. Carol was out of town, so Amanda had prevaricated when she'd told Jack she had other plans. She was only stretching the truth a little, though. After all, her plan was to get over Jack. According to her book, that meant reduced exposure.

Just as she was headed out the front door, she saw

Chloe Fortune and Mollie. "Hello, there. How's the wedding coming?"

"Slowly," Chloe said with a discouraged expression. "Mollie and I were supposed to meet Dad for lunch, but he's held up in meetings." She glanced at Amanda's newspaper. "Would you like to join us for a sandwich at Charlie's?"

"That would be nice. Thank you." Amanda had always admired Chloe's beauty and sense of style, and she couldn't deny the woman's warmth. "I love taking care of Lilly, but it's nice being around adults sometimes, too."

"That's right," Chloe said as the women walked the short block to the eatery. "You're the fill-in miracle nanny. Kate says you walk on water."

"That's definitely stretching it," Amanda said with a laugh. The three women followed the hostess to a small table in the corner of the busy restaurant.

"Has Jack seen the light and asked you to marry him?"

Amanda felt her cheeks heat. "Oh, no. Jack's definitely out of my league. In many ways," she added, thinking about his involvement with Trina. "What makes you say that?"

"Well, I think you might've mentioned something to Kelly, and she mentioned it to me and—" Chloe stopped and winced. "Forgive me for bringing it up."

Amanda immediately felt contrite. "I guess I didn't do a very good job keeping my unrequited—" she paused, not wanting to say the L word "—crush on Jack a secret. Some things have happened to make me see that it's time to move on. As a matter of fact, my karate instructor asked me out, and I think I'm going to go."

"Good idea," Mollie said.

"Definitely," Chloe agreed. "Although don't count Jack out. I think you would be so good for Jack."

Amanda's heart twisted. She had thought the same thing for a very long time. "I'm not sure Jack knows what he wants in a woman. In the meantime, it's silly for me to keep hoping when—" She needed to change the subject. "I need to get a haircut. I've always admired yours. Can you recommend a place?"

"You must go to Jacques at The Red Carpet Salon and Spa," Chloe insisted. "He's wonderful. Tell him I sent you. You ought to make Jack give you a day off and spend the whole day there getting pampered. After all you've done for him, he owes you."

"I could use a break," Amanda murmured.

"Then take one," Mollie said with a smile. Although Mollie was quite young, she seemed poised and mature for her age.

The waiter took their orders, then Mollie started discussing possibilities for Chloe and Mason's wedding reception.

Chloe sighed, frustration showing in her eyes. "I'm sorry, Mollie. I haven't had a chance to discuss any of this with my father or Mason. Mason has been busy lately. I feel as if I've been engaged forever. I wish everyone would stop getting married before me. Mason and I haven't even made love—" She closed her eyes and shook her head, wearing a weary smile. "Please forget you heard that."

The waiter delivered the drinks and knocked the

newspaper off the table, haphazardly scattering it. He apologized profusely and gathered it up, handing it to Amanda.

"Oh. There are the pictures from the benefit the other night in the Society section," Mollie said. "That must have been one incredible party."

"It was very nice," Chloe said, glancing at the paper. "It looks like the camera caught Gray McGuire. They're calling him the Bill Gates of Minneapolis."

"He's very good-looking," Mollie said. "Smart, good-looking, successful. Now that's the kind of man I wouldn't mind sweeping me off my feet."

Amanda heard the sounds of a romantic crush forming. She thought about warning Mollie, then nixed the idea. Although she couldn't tell it from her own experience, crushes were supposed to be fun as long as they were kept under control. She ripped out the picture of Gray McGuire and gave it to Mollie. "He's all yours."

Mollie laughed. "Okay. And you have fun on your date with your karate instructor."

Chloe gave Amanda a speculative glance. "Does Jack know about this date yet?"

"No. Why?"

Chloe smiled. "This could be interesting. You must call me after your date."

"Your hair is different," Jack said Saturday evening as Amanda returned a glass to the kitchen. She carried her new strappy sandals in her other hand.

Struggling with second thoughts about her date,

Amanda absently touched her hair. "Chloe recommended her stylist. I only had time for a cut."

Jack moved closer. "Looks nice," he said. "You look nice. Why the dress?" he asked in that silky voice that made her stomach knot.

Amanda took a deep breath and turned away. "I have a date."

"You have a *what?*"

Staring at the copper cookware on the étagère, Amanda cringed at his tone. "A date," she said. "It's when a man calls up a woman and invites her—"

"I know what a date is." His hand squeezed her shoulder, and he turned her around to face him. His green eyes searched hers. "What's going on?"

Amanda's heart pounded against her rib cage. From his look, she could almost think that the fact she was going on a date mattered to him. She swallowed. "My karate instructor asked me out."

"And you're going," he said in an incredulous voice.

She nodded.

"But you want me."

Amanda blinked. "I thought I did, but—"

"You *thought* you did?" he demanded, cocking his head to one side.

Her knees began to tremble. "I—I'm not sure we share the same—views on some issues."

"Amanda, what in hell are you talking about?"

Resenting his tone and her nervous reaction, she stiffened her spine. "I don't believe in trying to go to bed with one woman and dating another one at the same time."

"For the last time," he said, exasperation dripping from his tone, "what are you talking about?"

"You came on to me, told me I would ask you to make love to me, then went out with Trina." She lifted her hand when he opened his mouth. "That's fine. Not everyone shares my values. But I have no interest in being intimately involved with a man when the arrangement is not mutually exclusive. Call me crazy. Call me old-fashioned, but—"

Jack covered her mouth with his hand. "Trina asked me to take her to the benefit three weeks ago."

Feeling his hand on her lips, Amanda felt the bluster of her indignation wane. She stared into his eyes and felt a sinking sensation.

"Did you hear me?"

She nodded.

"Trina asked me to stay the night, but I didn't."

"Oh."

The doorbell rang. "Jeff!" she said. "I need to put on my shoes."

"You're not going with him," Jack said.

"Of course I'm going," Amanda said, bending down and struggling with the fasteners. "I agreed to go. I can't cancel now."

"I'll cancel for you," Jack offered.

Amanda rolled her eyes. "I'm not canceling."

"I don't want you to go."

Amanda's heart stopped. She looked at Jack, wondering how a statement that sounded like an order could have so much emotion in it. "It's just dinner. It would be wrong for me to cancel."

The doorbell rang again.

"I've got to go," she said.

"Okay," Jack said, but snagged her hand and drew her against him. He took her mouth with such passion and persuasion she nearly forgot her name. "I'll be waiting for you."

After he put Lilly to bed, Jack prowled the den. He had grossly underestimated and miscalculated where Amanda was concerned. He was paying for it now. Fair, he conceded to himself. It had been his mistake to view her as background music. He felt his jaw twitch in irritation. It had been arrogant of him to assume she wouldn't be able to fall out of love with him.

Amanda had more heart and backbone than any woman he'd ever met. If he weren't so totally disillusioned with the idea of romantic love, then maybe he could love her. He shook his head, rejecting the idea. He didn't believe romantic love existed for him anymore—even if his own brother now was a firm believer in it.

He did, however, believe in mutual passion. On a good day he could even see the possibility for mutual respect. He liked the way he felt when he was with Amanda. He liked how she was helping his daughter blossom.

He wanted her, and the intensity of his desire surprised him.

Glancing at the clock, he scowled. Why wasn't she home yet? The knowledge that she was out with another man stuck in his craw. When she'd left, Amanda had been wearing a dress that emphasized her slim, bare legs. Her hair was cut in a sexy style. After he'd kissed her, her brown eyes had glimmered with passion. *Jeff* probably hadn't been able to keep his hands off her.

Grinding his teeth, he deliberately pushed that thought aside. He'd never been involved with one of his employees. This would require some planning. Stalking across the carpet, he turned his attention to how he would handle the situation ethically.

Her shoes dangling from one hand, Amanda tiptoed through the front door just before midnight. The house was black except for a soft light in the kitchen. She glanced around for Jack and didn't see him. Just as well, she thought, breathing a sigh of relief. It had been a crazy night.

"Late night," he said from the darkness of the den.

Her heart raced. "His car broke down. It took forever to get a tow. He was so embarrassed I felt sorry for him. He finally called a cab for me to get home."

He stepped in front of her. "Did you have a good time?" he asked in a low voice.

"The restaurant he chose was very nice," she hedged. Her mind had been full of Jack.

"Did you like being with him?" he asked, standing very close.

"He was kind," she whispered, caught by the fire in his green eyes.

"Don't go out with him again." He cupped her cheek in his hand.

Fighting the way her heart was opening to him, she closed her eyes. "That sounds dictatorial."

"Did you think about how I kissed you?"

"Don't make me answer that."

"Did you?"

Feeling her resolve slip, she opened her eyes.

"Darn you, Jack Fortune! I was making progress. That was the first date I'd been on in a year. I'm trying to get over you."

"I don't want you to get over me," he said, sliding his arm around her and drawing her against him. "I want you," he said against her lips, then kissed her.

He gently, seductively consumed her mouth. He rubbed his mouth back and forth against hers, sucking her bottom lip into his mouth and exploring her with his tongue. His hard chest meshed with her breasts, turning her nipples into turgid points. He slid his hand lower to her bottom and guided her against him, making her intimately aware of his arousal.

She clung to him with her mouth and hands while her mind urged her to pull back. "We should stop," she said breathlessly. "You'll change your mind in the morning. You'll say we should keep our relationship professional."

Jack swept his tongue over her lips and beyond, denying her words. He tugged her dress upward and slid his hand beneath the silk of her panties to her bare skin and caressed her. With his other hand, he searched the curve of her breast and found her nipple with his thumb. He groaned in approval.

"We're not going to keep our relationship professional," he muttered.

Amanda felt Jack slide his fingers between her thighs, making her wet and swollen.

"Oh, you feel so good in my hands. We're not keeping our relationship professional," he repeated plunging his finger inside her. "I'm going to fire you," he said with a rough chuckle.

Her head in a fog, Amanda shivered and clenched around his caressing finger. *Fire you.* His words penetrated and she blinked, pushing at him. *"Fire me!"* Her knees wobbled. When she tried to step back, she stumbled.

Jack steadied her. "It was a joke, an exaggeration."

"You said the word *fire,*" she told him, and shook her head. "I can't give up my job. My sisters depend on me. I've made my way in life for a long time, and when you and I are done," she said, hating the hitch in her voice, "I'll continue to make my way."

"Reassign," Jack said, his gaze serious. "Things are different between us, and we can't go back. You can't be my assistant anymore. And believe me, that pains me to admit it, because you're the best damn assistant I've ever had. But every time you walk in my office now, I would be thinking about putting you on my desk and saying to hell with—" He stopped and cocked his head to one side, studying her. "You're blushing. Why?"

Amanda couldn't believe he'd just spoken her fantasy aloud. "I'm not."

"Yes, you are." He lifted his hands to cup her face. "Your cheeks are hot. Tell me what you're thinking at this very moment," he said.

She gulped. "I don't have to tell you."

"Tell me," he coaxed.

She sighed. "It's silly."

"Tell me."

Heavens, he was persistent. She looked away. "I used to think about your desk and wonder..." She couldn't finish.

"Wonder," he continued, his voice deepening in realization. "Wonder what it would be like for me to make love to you on that desk."

She gave a tiny nod.

Jack groaned and pulled her back into his arms. "Oh, Amanda, stay with me tonight."

Yes, yes, yes, her body and heart cried. She took a deep breath and swallowed.

"No."

Seven

"No," Amanda repeated as much for herself as him.

He went still, clearly unaccustomed to hearing the word *no*. "No?"

"No," she said again.

"Why?" he asked, his tone patient.

"Because it's too soon," she told him.

He pulled back and looked at her in disbelief.

"Jack, first I was invisible for over three years, then you wanted me for a few minutes. Then you wanted everything between us strictly professional. Now you want me in your bed." She blew her long bangs out of her eyes. "You've given me whiplash."

He looked at her for a long moment. "Are you saying I'm fickle?"

"If the size thirteen fits," she said.

He shook his head and gave a rough chuckle. "You

even know my shoe size. I've got a lot of catching up to do.''

She felt a stab of self-doubt. "I hope you're not disappointed," she said. "There's no big mystery here. I'm just a girl from North Carolina."

"And your shoe size is?" he asked.

"Seven and a half," Amanda said, and wondered how he could make such a question sound sexy. "Do you realize we've never been out on a date?"

Their first date was supposed to be at La Maison Restaurant, which boasted avant-garde French-Mediterranean fare and jazz music. The housekeeper had to cancel at the last minute because her son was sick, so she couldn't stay with Lilly. They went to Chuck E. Cheese instead, which boasted pizza and dancing bears.

Lilly loved it.

"This is not what I planned," Jack said above the din of what seemed like a million screaming kids. "A Minnesota Twins game is more peaceful than this."

"Welcome to the life of the single dad," Amanda said with a smile. "The cuisine is definitely different."

"More noise."

"More purple-fruit-punch kisses," she told him, nodding toward Lilly, who was swinging from side to side in her booster seat.

He saw the happiness on Lilly's face and felt something inside him ease. "Good point." He reached for Amanda's hand. "I don't know many women who would put up with this as a first date."

Amanda eyed him thoughtfully. "Maybe you haven't been moving in the right circles."

Maybe not, Jack realized. Her slow drawl slid under his skin, making him wonder for the hundredth time how he could have been so blind where she was concerned. Kate's comment echoed through his mind again. *Amanda would make a great mother, a great wife....*

The bears took an intermission break, and Lilly turned around. "Wanna play the favorites game, Daddy?" she asked. "'Manda told me it in the doctor's office."

"Okay," he said, although he was clueless. "What's the favorites game?"

"You name a subject, then guess each other's favorites," Amanda said. "Like favorite color. Lilly, you start. Think of your favorite color and let your dad guess."

"Pink," Jack said.

Lilly shook her head. "Purple. Now think of your favorite color, Daddy."

Jack nodded. "Okay."

"Red," Lilly said.

"Blue." Amanda's lips twitched.

"Blue," he confirmed, feeling a buzz when he thought about how much she knew about him. "You knew. Why am I not surprised? Okay, mystery woman, what's *your* favorite color? Green," he guessed.

Amanda shook her head.

"Rainbow!" Lilly said.

"You remembered," Amanda said and kissed his

daughter's cheek. "That's right. I can't pick just one. My favorite color changes with the day."

They continued with sports, and Jack learned that Amanda once again knew his favorite—fly-fishing. Lilly's was karate, and he successfully guessed swimming for Amanda. The amused surprise in her eyes made him hungry to know more. Later that night, after Lilly was tucked in her bed, Jack led Amanda into the den, put on a saxophone CD and pulled her into his arms. He continued the favorites game.

"Favorite music," he prompted.

"Depending on your mood, your favorite is a combination of the hard rock of your youth, and New Age instrumentals to dissolve your tension."

Curious about her thoughts, he tugged at her hair. "What's a hard rock mood?"

"Conquest," she told him with a sensual, knowing look in her eyes. "Hard rock is when you're out to conquer the world."

In that case, he should have hard rock on right now, Jack thought, because he wanted to conquer Amanda. "How did you know that?"

"Years of observation," she muttered.

"And your favorite is—" He swore under his breath. He had no idea. "Classical."

She pulled back and wrinkled her nose. "Not really. I like Vonda Sheppard and Bonnie Raitt."

"Okay," he said, tucking the information in his brain.

"I like The Wallflowers and—" she shook her head "—I'm not sure I'm ready to tell you this. It's a secret."

He wondered how she managed to be so innocently

sexy. "Then you have to tell. I should know all your secrets."

"You're sure," she said, looking at him as if she were assessing whether he could *take* it or not.

"I'm sure."

"Elvis."

He laughed. "You're kidding."

"I'm not. I was indoctrinated at a young age. My mother loved Elvis. She even said she once kissed him after a concert. I believe her, but I'm not sure the rest of the world would. She required us to watch his movies and I remember sighing over his romantic songs."

"Ah, a romantic," he said, feeling a rush of cynicism, but forgiving her naiveté. She hadn't had her heart blown apart like he had. A part of him hoped she never would. He lowered his lips to hers and gently took her mouth. Her soft sigh rubbed at his heart. He rested his forehead against hers. "Amanda, you worked by my side day in and day out for years. How did I miss you?"

"Do you want the truth?"

"Yes."

"There are two theories. One is that an evil witch put a spell on you and blinded you so you couldn't see me."

He nodded at that notion, as fanciful as it sounded. His wife could have been the evil witch. "And the other theory?"

Her eyes darkened with doubt. "Maybe I'm better at being invisible than being visible."

Amanda and Carol skipped their lunch date to shop. Carol's current love interest was an artist. She wanted a campy outfit so she would fit in at his ex-hibit. "What do you think of this?" Carol asked, pull-ing from the rack a loose black dress with abstract colored swirls of pumpkin and eggplant.

"It's distinctive," Amanda said, hedging.

"Okay, you've given the polite response. What do you really think?"

Amanda winced. "It looks like Lilly got hold of some expired finger paints and painted it. Blind-folded," she added, thinking Lilly would produce a prettier work.

"You've been hanging around three-year-olds too long. When are you going back to work with Jack?"

Amanda's stomach tightened. "I don't think I am."

Carol stuck the dress back on the rack, doing a double take. "Why not?"

"We're involved," she said. "Sort of."

"Sort of," Carol echoed.

Amanda fanned through another round of dresses to avoid Carol's intense curiosity. "We're involved, so he is going to reassign me when I come back to work."

"Have you gone to bed with him?"

Amanda felt her cheeks heat. Things got very warm for them outside her bedroom door every night. "No, but he wants to."

"Then why haven't you? Isn't he your dream man."

"Yes, he's my dream man." Amanda's stomach twisted in another knot. She didn't feel she could be totally open about her worries to anyone, even Carol. "I'm different from the other women Jack has been involved with. I'm afraid I may disappoint him. I'm not as experienced," she said quietly, knowing that was a gross understatement.

Carol lifted an eyebrow. "Sounds like the fantasy's different from the reality."

"In some ways," Amanda agreed. "I knew him as a boss. Getting to know him as a man is different. He's still the most exciting man I've ever met, but…"

"I'm all for fantasy, Amanda. And fantasy's easy. In our minds we can make a situation turn out any way we want. It takes real guts and courage to make reality work." Carol smiled wryly. "Which is why I'm looking for a fantasy dress at the moment."

"Guts and courage," Amanda repeated under her breath like a mantra, as she pulled her late-model economy car into Jack's four-car garage beside his Mercedes. The difference between her and Jack could be sharply drawn even between their cars.

"Guts and courage," she said again, feeling a shortage of both. Despite the differences between Jack and her, Amanda had a sense of fate about him that went beyond her fantasy. Something inside her told her that he needed *her*. She wanted, she so wanted, to be his.

Something also told her it wasn't going to be a smooth road to win Jack's heart. That was why she'd done everything she could today to bolster her courage. She'd even gone to an extra karate lesson.

Walking through the garage to the kitchen, she cursed her jitters. Jack appeared in the doorway, and her heart stopped.

"Hi," she said.

"Hi," he returned. His shirt was open, his hair slightly mussed by his fingers, she guessed, and his eyes held hers. "The housekeeper gave me your message. Karate?"

Amanda nodded, growing more nervous by the moment. She touched her hair. "I took a shower afterward."

"Did Jeff teach the class?" he asked with strained casual interest.

"Yes, he teaches a lot of the beginner classes." She paused, thinking Jack couldn't possibly be jealous of Jeff. "I don't want him," she told him, meeting his gaze.

He looked at her for a long, silent moment filled with anticipation, then pulled her against him. "Who do you want, Amanda?" he asked, and kissed her.

Her head began to spin. She inhaled his masculine scent and clung to the strength of his body. She tasted passion and possessiveness in his tongue, and the combination only made her more dizzy.

He pulled back slightly and slid his fingers through her damp hair, changing the angle of her mouth against his. "Answer the question. Who do you want?"

"You," she said breathlessly, her heart hammering in her chest. "You."

"When?"

Sliding his knee between her trembling legs, the word was more a sensual demand than question. Fear, excitement and determination battled for control. This was meant to be. She closed her eyes.

"Now."

The room spun as he swung her into his arms.

He carried her up the stairs to his room, letting her slowly slide down the length of his body while he took her mouth with a dark wanting. His mouth was hot on hers, his chest hard where she clung to him. She barely had time to register each new sensation. She felt his heart beating against her palm, inhaled his clean masculine scent and felt the possessiveness in his hands.

A second seemed to pass and her blouse and bra were gone. Another second, and she felt his hands on her cotton shorts.

Her stomach dipped with arousal and nervousness. She pulled her mouth away and swallowed. "I'm not like the other women you've known," she said, warning him, preparing him for her lack of experience.

His gaze dipped from her face to her breasts and lower. "I'm glad." He backed up to the bed, sitting down, then boldly took her small breast in his mouth while he pushed her shorts and panties down her hips.

He slid his hand between her legs to where she was wet and wanting. "I want inside you," he said in a guttural tone. "I want to feel you wet and tight all around me."

Squeezing her bottom, he pressed openmouthed kisses down her abdomen and thighs. Amanda was a sea of want and nerves, more want than nerves. Jack looked up at her and fell back on the bed, his eyes laser hot with passion.

He urged her knees on the bed and pulled her up, up, up until his mouth took her intimately. Amanda gasped at how he was caressing her. Self-conscious, yet sensually curious, she closed her eyes. His tongue sent a thousand shuddering sensations through her. Amanda swallowed a moan.

Jack gently rolled her on her side and pushed down his jeans. "You're so sweet," he muttered. "Touch me, Amanda," he said, guiding her hand to him.

She would do anything to answer the need in his voice. Amanda stroked him while he caressed her. Burning with an ache for him, she felt her control slip away. She felt the contrast of his soft chest hair and muscular chest against her breasts, his hard thigh sliding between hers. She couldn't get close enough.

He grabbed a packet from his bedside table and quickly protected her. Poised over her, he pushed her thighs apart and devoured her with his gaze. "Hold on," he said, then thrust inside her.

Amanda gasped at the invasion, the twinge of being stretched too quickly.

Jack stared at her, his gaze surprised, unsettled. "You're not—" He broke off when she moved and groaned in pleasure. "You're so tight, too tight. Oh, Amanda."

Her body adjusted to his, and she tentatively wiggled. She felt hot, excited and full. Arching slightly beneath him, she licked her dry lips and watched him shudder.

"Amanda, stop." He clasped his hands around her hips. "You're not a virgin."

"I'm not a virgin," she whispered, feeling the pleasure rise inside her again. "Not anymore. I want to move," she said, instinctively arching toward him again. "I want you to move."

"Not anymore." The muscles in his arms and shoulders straining, Jack bowed his head and swore.

"Okay, sweetheart," he said and began to pump in long fluid strokes.

Amanda shivered around him. She felt the tension inside her tighten with each movement. Tighter, higher, she was reaching. She felt as if she were climbing to the top of a cliff. If she reached the top, she would fly. She knew it. She stretched, closer, then reached it.

Jack gave a wild groan, his powerful body quaking in and around her. His pleasure washed over her like the tide, and Amanda savored every sensation.

He dipped his head in the hollow of her shoulder, his breath warm on her skin. "Why didn't you tell me you were a virgin?"

Amanda was still savoring him and the rhythmic tension pulsing inside her. Her mind was a delicious haze. "I—I tried. I told you I was different from the other women you knew."

"Why didn't you tell me?"

The hint of disapproval in his voice cut through her euphoria.

He lifted his head and moved slightly away from her. In his gaze she saw distrust.

The warmth drained away from her. Confused, she could only stare at him.

"I don't want to think that you tricked me."

Amanda felt a chill. "Tricked you?" she echoed. "How could I—" She swallowed. "Why should I—"

"Some women would try to get pregnant, then surprise me."

She shook her head in confusion. "Why would I do that? Why?"

"So I would be forced to marry you," he said. "The way I was forced to marry Sandra."

Jack rolled to the side of the bed and stared into the darkness.

Shock rolled through her. Amanda couldn't remember feeling so empty and vulnerable. She could sense his hurt and wanted badly to reach out to him, but he seemed so far away. With trembling hands, she groped for her blouse and shorts. She was so stunned she couldn't even cry. "I went to see a doctor today and went on the pill. He said I should use another form of contraception for a month, so I got a diaphragm." She laughed, and the sound was incredibly sad to her own ears. "I had decided I wanted to be with you tonight. It was right to be with you. It had never really felt right before. I put the diaphragm in after karate. It took me a long time. That's why I was late."

Her fingers too numb to allow her to fasten her clothes, she gave up and struggled to her feet. Heaven help her, any minute she was going to cry. "I need to leave. I really need to leave."

Eight

Jack moved in front of her, naked, strong, his eyes full of regret. He raked his hands through his hair. "Don't go. I was wrong."

At a loss, Amanda searched, but couldn't find any words.

His nostrils flared. "I learned one of your secrets tonight. You learned one of mine. Not many people know Sandra was pregnant before we married. My marriage taught me some lasting lessons. I don't trust easily. I don't believe in fairy tales. I don't believe in happily-ever-after anymore. But that's no excuse to be harsh toward you." He shook his head. "I'm sorry. Stay."

It was almost too much for her to comprehend at the moment. Her body was still trembling from making love, and her mind was reeling with what he'd revealed about his marriage. "I—I think it would be better if I go to my room."

He put his hands on her arms. "Amanda, this was your first time. I've been a bastard. Let me make it better. Stay with me."

She swallowed over the lump in her throat and looked at his big bed. "I don't think—"

He skimmed his hand down her bare arm and took her by the hand. "This isn't about sex. Come here. I'll run a bath for you."

He led her into his plush master bath, gently urged her into a small brass chair, and turned on the jets to the deep tub. "Stay there," he said. "I'll be back in a minute."

True to his word, he returned clad in a silk robe and carrying a glass of wine. He took off her clothes with the same care he would show a child.

His tenderness made something inside her ease, and she took a deep breath as she sank into the tub. The warm water soothed her body and spirit. Jack handed her the wine.

"Do you want something to eat?"

She shook her head and sipped the wine. "Another first," she murmured. "I've never taken a bath in front of a man."

He entwined his fingers through hers. "You're a sexy, warm woman, Amanda. I have to ask. How in the world did you keep from getting sexually involved until now?"

She sighed. "You may not understand this, but the time and the person just never matched up until you. My mother was a single parent, and she depended on me when I was a teenager. I went to college for two years, but I lived at home. Then my mother died, and in order to keep the family together, I couldn't give Social Services any reason to think I wasn't the best choice as guardian for my brother and sisters.''

Jack cocked his head to the side thoughtfully, and Amanda felt her heart dip. A simple habit, she thought, but when he did it, she couldn't remain unaffected.

''You've been in Minneapolis for a few years, now,'' he ventured.

''I dated some, when I first moved here,'' she said. ''But every day at the office, there was you. Nobody I met could compare.'' She took another sip of wine. ''You ruined me.''

His lips twitched. ''What about me caught your attention?''

Amanda rolled her eyes. ''What didn't? You already know you're incredibly good-looking. I was fascinated by your confidence and energy. You were intense about everything you did, and you *made* things happen. I had never met someone so driven.'' She paused, remembering gentler moments. ''But I also saw how you helped an employee get into rehab instead of just firing him. I saw you long for your daughter,'' she said, her eyes growing misty. ''I didn't stand a chance.''

He cupped her cheek with his hand. ''Come back to bed with me.''

Amanda tensed. ''I don't think Lilly should find me in your bed in the morning. It might be confusing for her.''

''Then I'll come to your room. I'll set the alarm

and leave before she wakes up. I'm not leaving you alone tonight.''

Jack led her to her bed, and Amanda fell asleep in his arms, thinking if this was reality, it was better than all her fantasies.

The following morning, Jack awakened to the sound of his alarm. Quickly turning it off, he watched Amanda sleeping. Her face held the innocence of a child's, yet he knew from personal experience that she loved like a woman, like no other woman he'd known.

Knowing she'd given him her virginity made him feel protective of her. He would never forgive himself for how he'd treated her when he'd first discovered her inexperience. Even now, he couldn't believe the force of his reaction to being deceived and *caught* again. He hated that Sandra's deception still ate at him.

Amanda was nothing like her, he thought, touching her soft hair. If his heart hadn't been hollowed out, he could have loved her. He wondered if it was wrong to take her love when he knew he would never love her back. Jack frowned. No fairy tales in his future. When it came to true love, his heart had turned to stone.

''I know this is short notice,'' Jack told Amanda as she watched Lilly in the backyard, ''but my mother wants to see her grandchild. She'd like us to come for dinner.''

Amanda shrugged. ''It shouldn't be a problem.

Lilly took her nap today. I can get her dressed and ready to go with you in no time.''

Jack paused and dropped a kiss on her mouth. ''I want you to go with us.''

Amanda's stomach dipped. ''Why?''

''Lilly would be more comfortable, and I think my parents are curious about you. They only know you as my 'invisible' assistant.''

Realization hit. ''Kate,'' Amanda said.

''Kate,'' he said with a nod. ''And Chloe, and me.''

She felt a rush of pleasure at the notion that Jack was talking about her. ''I don't know what to say.''

''That's easy,'' he said with a thigh-melting smile. ''Say yes,'' he said in a voice that spelled trouble, ''to everything I ask.''

''You're spoiled,'' she told him. ''You're used to me being at your beck and call all day long. You've grown accustomed to me saying yes.''

''That's right. Not having you around makes me cranky.''

Amanda's lips twitched. ''Okay. Uncle. I'll go. Did I thank you for hugging me to sleep last night?''

''No,'' he said, seductively crowding her. ''It could happen again.''

He was warm and wonderful against her. Amanda felt herself turn to liquid.

''When I look in your eyes, I almost think you would make love to me right here in the kitchen.''

Amanda's breath stalled and she glanced downward. If her eyes could talk, then they were saying entirely too much. ''If you want me to go to your parents I need to get Lilly and me ready.''

"I'll let you go," he said, "this time."

An hour later they pulled up the brick-paved drive to Stuart and Marie Fortune's impressive two-story stone house overlooking the lake.

"It's beautiful," Amanda said. "The setting is so serene."

"It suits them both," Jack said helping her and Lilly out of the car.

Marie, a well-groomed, gently aging and attractive woman, opened the door before they'd finished climbing the steps. "Omigoodness," she said, clasping her hands together. "Lilly, you've grown a foot taller."

Lilly held tight to Amanda's hand. Literally feeling the child's tension, Amanda kneeled close to her. "You haven't seen your nana Fortune in a long time. Look at her smile. It's just like your daddy's, and yours, too."

Lilly peeked up at Marie and gave a shy smile. "She's pretty," Lilly whispered.

Marie's eyes filled with tears, and she reached out to gently embrace her granddaughter. "Thank you, both of you," she said, looking at Jack and Amanda, "for bringing her to see us. Come in. Dinner's ready."

The house was as elegantly tasteful and warm as Marie. Amanda could see Jack's mother's personality in the quietly beautiful furnishings. The evidence of family was strong, with photographs displayed of Jack and his brother Garrett at various stages of development.

Although Amanda had met Jack's father, Stuart, at the office, the resemblance between father and son struck her anew. She noticed Stuart was particularly attentive to Marie throughout the evening. At the same time, Amanda thought he seemed somewhat distracted.

After dinner Lilly was still whispering. Jack tugged her hair and whispered something in her ear.

"Here?" Lilly asked.

Jack nodded. "Lilly's been taking karate, and she's going to show you a few things she's learned."

In her ruffled dress with the purple sash, Lilly balled her small fists and stood in fighting stance, then let out a loud *"Kiyah!"*

Startled, but delighted, Stuart and Marie applauded, and Amanda fell a little more in love with Jack for helping break the ice for his daughter. After a few more exhibition punches and kicks, Lilly's whisper was gone.

"Dad," Jack said, "let's take a walk in the yard. I want to get your opinion on something. We'll be back soon," he said to Amanda and Lilly.

"Business," Marie said with a glint of worry in her eyes, as her husband and son left the room. "Stuart has been…" Her voice trailed off and she glanced back at Amanda. "That's fine. It means I get a few extra minutes with my granddaughter."

Lilly stood quietly twisting her hands for a long moment. Sensing Lilly's discomfort and Marie's eagerness, Amanda silently mouthed the word *cookie* to Marie.

Recognition dawned in her eyes and she nodded. "Would you like a cookie, sweetheart?"

Lilly's face brightened. "Yes ma'am. 'Manda says

I'm a cookie monster. 'Cept I'm not blue. I just like cookies.''

Marie led them back to the kitchen where she gave Lilly a cookie and received a hug for the small treat. Marie's eyes were misty as she turned to Amanda. "You've done such a nice job with her. Jack told us how sad Lilly was when she first came to his house. I wanted to be here, but Stuart and I were out of the country. Thank you for helping my grandbaby find her sparkle again," she said and embraced Amanda.

Amanda felt her own eyes burn with emotion. "It was easy to fall for her. I see Jack every time I look in her eyes."

Marie gave her a searching glance. "You've been good for Jack, too. He was so hurt when his marriage broke up. I've been worried about him. Maybe with you—"

Amanda's stomach clenched and she shook her head. "Oh there's nothing like that. Nothing permanent between Jack and me," she said, feeling an ache at the truth of her statement.

Marie's brow knit in confusion. "Are you sure? The way he looks at you…" She shrugged. "Well, whatever you've done has worked for my son and my granddaughter, and I'll always be grateful."

"It's been my pleasure," Amanda said, suddenly realizing that giving up Lilly's care would soon be a reality and a big part of her wasn't looking forward to it.

Jack and his father walked in the back door, their faces slightly pensive. Jack looked at Lilly and Amanda and grinned. "Nana found out we have a cookie monster in the family."

Lilly giggled.

"What have you two been talking about?" Marie asked, walking toward Stuart. "Did one of your stocks take a wrong turn on the market? You look gloomy."

"I insulted Dad on his golf game," Jack said. "We haven't played in a while. Now he's plotting when to pulverize me on the course."

Marie put her arm around her husband. "You two!" she said and kissed his cheek.

Amanda saw Stuart cover her hand tightly with his. They clearly loved each other, but something didn't feel right. She glanced at Jack and saw just a tiny bit of stiffness in the smile that didn't reach his eyes.

"We should leave," Jack said. "Dinner was great."

"Oh, no. So soon?" Marie said.

Amanda brushed the crumbs off of Lilly's hands and lifted her out of the chair. "If you'd like, I can bring Lilly to visit again sometime soon."

"I would love that. Please call me," Marie said.

Stuart reached out to shake Amanda's hand. "It was nice meeting you in a personal setting. Kate and Jack have had nothing but praise for you. Now, I know why."

Amanda felt her cheeks heat from the attention. "Thank you," she murmured, and was relieved to feel the cool air on her face when they walked outside to Jack's car.

Within five minutes Lilly was asleep in her car seat as Jack drove home.

"Your parents are lovely," Amanda said to Jack.

"They liked you, too. My mother may be ready to

erect a statue in your honor since Lilly gave her a hug,'' he said tongue in cheek.

Amanda chuckled. "It was a bit much," she admitted. "But I was impressed. Your parents seem very devoted to each other."

Jack's face tightened slightly. "They appreciate what they have. They know how to protect it," he said, and added, "now."

Silence followed, and Amanda sensed Jack's disquiet. "Are you okay?"

"Yes," he said. "I'm fine."

"Are you sure? You seem distracted or bothered."

He shrugged. "No more than usual."

Amanda disagreed, but said nothing. His tension was so thick she could feel it between them like a thick curtain. She wanted to reach out. She didn't want him to feel alone, but she didn't want to intrude, either.

For the rest of the drive home, they were silent. Amanda changed a sleepy Lilly into pajamas and tucked her into bed. After she and Jack dropped kisses on Lilly's forehead, they walked into the hallway.

Jack seemed as if he carried a heavy weight on his broad shoulders. Amanda knew he was strong. He could handle whatever came his way. He certainly didn't need her help. In the back of her mind, though, she heard Carol's message. *Reality is harder than fantasy.*

"I think everyone counts on you to be sane and strong," she said softly.

His guarded gaze met hers.

"I know you're strong, but I've watched you and cared about you too long not to know when something is bothering you." She lifted her hand when his jaw tightened and he opened his mouth. "You don't have to tell me what it is. I just want you to know that if you get tired of being alone with it, I'm here for you." Taking her courage in her hands, she stretched up on her toes and kissed his cheek. "Good night."

An hour later Jack prowled his bedroom, restless, nowhere near sleep. After his father had confessed his long-ago affair, Jack had enlisted the help of a trustworthy security consultant to learn if there was, indeed, any threat to his father. He'd received a call today that there might be some suspicious movement in his father's company's stock. His father, a true maverick at heart, kept a finger in the Fortune pie and sat on the board, but had spent his life building Knight Star Systems.

The company had been his third child, Jack thought, and his father's extreme devotion to Knight Star Systems may have caused marital problems. Although his father was still a force to reckon with, the idea that someone was financially stalking him made Jack want to punch something.

He wouldn't, though. He had learned a man had to use his best defenses in these matters. A clear head would serve him and his father best.

He was concerned for his father. He was bothered by Amanda. He eyed the clock. Midnight. Deciding to grab today's paper from the den and read it until he fell asleep, he pulled on his robe and left his room. As he passed Amanda's room, he noticed her light was still on. He went downstairs to get the paper, and on his way back he paused at her door.

Her light was still on, and he knew she would welcome him in her heart if not in her bed. He'd been unable to conceal his turmoil, and that bothered the hell out of him.

He tapped lightly on her door, and entered when she answered. She lay propped against pillows with a book on her lap.

It crossed his mind that she had been waiting for him. Crazy, he thought, but he couldn't shake the feeling. She reminded him of a candle in the window. He'd never had that kind of woman in his life. He'd never thought he wanted that kind of woman in his life. He couldn't, however, deny the whisper of peace that drifted through him just looking at her.

Jack frowned.

"Was there something specific you wanted or were you just planning to scowl at me?" she asked sweetly.

If he weren't so restless, he might have been amused. "It bothers me that you can read me so well. I'm not used to having a woman care about me the way you do."

She nodded. "Would you like me to stop?"

Nine

Amanda's question stopped him in his tracks. *Would you like me to stop?* The possibility of her *stopping* chipped out a small empty place in his chest. It wasn't his heart, he thought. Surely she couldn't be affecting his heart. For a moment he wondered if it was an ulcer. Was it possible that sweet Amanda could give him an ulcer?

Her quiet confidence tugged at something deep inside him. She drew him like a candle in the window. Maybe it was time for him to go toward the light instead of away from it.

"No," he finally said, moving toward her and lifting her hand to his lips. "I don't want you to stop."

She tugged him down to the bed and smiled. "Sometimes it was easier loving you in secret."

"Maybe I need to make it more rewarding." He

checked the title of her book before he pulled it off her lap. *Inside the Three-Year-Old Mind*? He shook his head. "You're such a jewel, Amanda. It's a wonder you haven't kicked me in the rear."

"My ankle's still sore," she deadpanned. "But I'm sure it will recover."

He grinned.

She grinned, too, then her expression turned thoughtful. "You are accustomed to beautiful women, Jack. I'm not beautiful."

His instinct was to deny it immediately, but he wanted to give her a better answer, an answer that would take the doubt away from her. "There's superficial beauty and there's inner beauty," he began.

She rolled her eyes. "Oh, don't tell me I'm pretty on the inside and that's where it counts."

"You are beautiful on the inside, but it shows through on the outside. In your eyes," he said, lifting his hand to her cheek, "in your smile, in the way you move."

He met her gaze. "And the way you want me makes me want to make love to you all the time."

Her eyes widened, and her cheeks turned pink. "Really?"

"Really," he said, taking her mouth and knowing deep in his gut he wasn't the right man for her. She deserved a man with a heart, and Jack knew he didn't have one. But she loved him, and her sweet sensuality filled an empty place inside him. Her devotion was more seductive than anything he'd ever faced.

"I'm not right for you," he said, giving her the only warning he could. She was soft and warm, utterly responsive to him. He slipped his hands beneath her gown and felt her nipples harden beneath her touch; her heart raced against his palm. Was there anything more seductive than Amanda's obvious desire for him? His blood heated and pooled in his loins. "I can't resist you. Do you want me to stop?"

Her breath hitched, and the sound might as well have been an intimate caress from her hand.

"No," she whispered, arching against him. "Don't stop."

Delilah scampered to Jack the second he walked in the door from the airport after returning from a short business trip. She wrapped herself around his leg until he dropped his suitcase and petted her. As he walked toward the back of the house, he overheard Amanda and Lilly in the kitchen.

"Three care packages," Amanda said, and there was a rustling of paper. "My sisters and brother will be glad to get these."

"Do you send cookies every time?" Lilly asked in a voice muffled, Jack suspected, by a cookie.

"Every time," Amanda said. "When I was in college, I didn't have anyone to send me cookies, so I always wanted to make sure my sisters and brother got a little extra TLC sometimes. Can you think of someone else who could use some TLC?"

Silence followed. "Daddy. He's been workin' hard."

"Great idea," Amanda said. "You are brilliant. Did you know that? Beautiful and brilliant and kind."

Jack's chest tightened at the conversation. His three-year-old daughter had thought of doing something nice for him. Amanda was teaching Lilly things he would have never considered. His life had been turned upside down in the past months. His house was littered with toys, his refrigerator covered with Lilly's pictures, and the woman in his life gave him peace at the same time she quietly haunted him when he was away from her. God knows, he wasn't comfortable with all the changes, but at this moment, he wouldn't change a thing.

He strode into the kitchen. "Do I smell cookies?"

Amanda swung around from the kitchen table and smiled. Dressed in shorts and a cropped top, she looked casual and sexy. His gaze fell to her long, slim legs, and he remembered how they felt wrapped around him. "You're home early," she said, her eyes lighting in welcome.

"Daddy!" Lilly ran across the room to give him a hug. Jack dropped his attaché case and swung her up in his arms, heedless of the cookie crumbs she rubbed on him.

"Have you been busy?" he asked her.

She nodded. "Helpin' 'Manda make care packages for her sisters and brother 'cause their mom died like mine. 'Cept I don't need a care package 'cause I got you and 'Manda and Delilah and I'm not in college yet."

Jack blinked at Lilly's reply. That was the most she'd ever said to him since she'd come to live with him. He grinned. "Sounds like you've got it figured out. On the way home from the airport, I brought some videos for you to watch with the housekeeper tonight while I take Amanda out for a grown-up dinner." He glanced at Amanda and saw a look of surprised pleasure cross her face.

Lilly pursed her little rosebud mouth. "What are the videos?"

"I think she may have inherited her negotiational skills from the Fortune side," Amanda murmured.

Jack had done his research with the video clerk. He named the contents of his stash, and the movies met with Lilly's approval.

"Can I watch them now?"

"May I please watch them after my bath?" Amanda prompted.

Lilly echoed her, and Jack ruffled her hair. "Yes, you may."

Lilly skipped off to her room, and Jack turned to Amanda, who was taping the packages. "So, no one ever sent you a care package?" he asked.

She gave him a sideways glance. "You were eavesdropping."

"No, your cat detained me against my will at the door, and I overheard you."

Amanda's lips twitched. "That, I believe."

"I thought you said you went to college for two years before your mother died," he said, helping himself to one of the cookies on the plate.

"I commuted because it was less expensive, and my mom still needed help."

Jack thought about the devotion his parents had showered on him throughout his growing-up years. He had never lacked for anything.

The silence seemed to make her uncomfortable. "It's not a big deal," she said. "My background may be very different from yours, but it's not really that unusual. I think I turned out okay."

The sliver of defensiveness in her tone made him

grin. He pulled her into his arms. "You turned out better than okay. I just thought you deserved to have some TLC along the way."

He looked down at her, and the odd thought struck him that he would like to give that to Amanda. Jack had been so focused on work during the past few years that he'd never thought about taking care of anyone else. He thought of the jeweler's box in his attaché. Was he changing?

Dismissing the thought as too complicated, he lowered his mouth to hers for a long kiss that made him want to take her up to his bedroom. "I'm surprised at you, Amanda. You were never tardy for work."

She wrinkled her brow in confusion. "Tardy?"

"I've been home more than five minutes, and you haven't thrown yourself at me, telling me you've been counting the minutes when I would arrive."

She laughed and shook her head. "I didn't know that was a job requirement. I don't have a lot of experience in *throwing myself* at men. I may need some training."

"I'll train you," he said, breathing in the combined scent of sugar, vanilla and Amanda. "First, you kiss me," he told her.

She lifted her lips to his and rubbed them back and forth in a slow rhythm that made his blood heat.

"Then you rub your breasts against my chest," he whispered.

Amanda did as he instructed, and Jack felt himself grow hard. Instinctively she undulated against him, and he lowered his hands to her bottom, guiding her. Her tongue tangled with his in a surprisingly carnal kiss.

Jack remembered how good she felt naked beneath him, as he thrust inside her. He groaned, remembering they were in the kitchen. Lilly could walk in any minute. He reluctantly pulled away. "You learn quickly."

She took a shaky breath, revealing her own arousal. "You are an excellent teacher."

The look in her eyes said she would have let him take her on the kitchen table. Jack reined in his overwhelming desire to do just that. "I wanted to give you a thank-you and TLC dinner out tonight. Since I've been out of town the last few days, you've been stuck in the castle," he said. "Plus I've missed being alone with you."

Her gaze deepened with emotion. "I think I like that reason best."

A couple of hours later, Amanda sat with Jack in a table tucked into the corner of The 510 Restaurant. Originally a turn-of-the-century apartment-hotel, the exclusive restaurant exuded an elegant ambience with high ceilings, chandeliers and Queen Anne chairs.

Amanda sipped her wine and tried to relax. It was difficult with Jack's attention devoted totally to her. "How did you manage reservations?"

"I called from the plane," he said, "and the owners know me."

"It's beautiful," she said.

"Yes, and the food and service are great. A good escape from the castle," he said with a grin.

"Yes," she agreed and wondered how long Jack would stay interested in her. Amanda had spent a lot of time wondering about that during the past week.

"That reminds me. I'm thinking of taking Lilly to a play group. It's time for her to make some little friends."

"You think she's ready?"

"If I stay with her the first time, I think she'll be okay. It crossed my mind that she shouldn't get too attached to me since you'll be getting a permanent nanny and I'll come back to work."

Jack frowned. "I hadn't considered that."

"I don't know who it's going to be more difficult for—Lilly or me. I'm just as attached to her as she is to me."

"There's no rush for you to leave," Jack said, reaching for her hand. "More than one Fortune likes having you at our house."

Her stomach dipped. "And I like being there for both of you," she murmured.

"Jack Fortune," a male voice called. "It's been a while."

Jack glanced up at a couple approaching their table. Amanda spotted the red-haired woman and thought she looked familiar.

Jack stood. "Ken, Trina, it's good to see you," he said shaking the man's hand. "This is Amanda Corbain. Ken Dearborn and Trina Sullivan."

Amanda shook hands and greeted them both. Trina edged closer while Jack and Ken talked.

"I've heard your name before. I just can't place it," the sophisticated red-haired woman said. She closed her eyes for a second, then opened them. "Jack's secretary," she said. "You're Jack's secretary."

"Yes, I was," Amanda said, feeling awkward under the woman's curious gaze. "I've had a change of assignment. I'm taking care of Jack's daughter for a little while."

Realization crossed Trina's face. "Oh, his daughter." She made a tsking sound. "Such a shame about Sandra's accident. Is her daughter as pretty as she was?"

"At least as pretty. Lilly's a joy," Amanda said.

"Well, I know Jack's daughter is very important to him. If you're taking care of her, then I know you're important to him, too," she said with a too-bright smile.

The waiter appeared with their meal.

"We should go," Ken said. "Don't be a stranger, Jack. It was nice meeting you, Amanda."

After they left, the waiter served their meal. Distracted by Trina's comments, Amanda silently ate.

"You're too quiet," Jack said. "What did Trina say?"

Her stomach tightened. "Just small talk. It took her a moment to remember I was your secretary."

He nodded. "I'm sure she was quick to remind you of your place."

Amanda thought about denying it, but smiled instead. "She was somewhat subtle about it. She was eyeing my wine, so I guess I'm lucky she didn't dump it in my lap. She's not happy to lose you."

"She didn't ever really have me," Jack said bluntly.

"Who has?" Amanda asked.

Jack lifted his eyebrow. "Pardon?"

Amanda resisted the urge to feel intimidated beneath his intent gaze. "Who has really had you?"

He put his wineglass down and glanced away, then back at her, his gaze wry, yet thoughtful. "That's a good question." He took her hand. "You make me think."

"Is that good or bad?"

He lifted her hand to his lips. "Ultimately good. I'm just not used to it."

Even though he hadn't really answered her question, Amanda felt as if he'd been honest with her, and it made her feel closer to him. They finished their entrées and listened to the waiter recite the choices for dessert.

Jack nodded toward her. "What would you like?"

"They all sound delicious, but I've had enough."

He turned back to the waiter and asked for the check. Jack looked at her. "I have something I want to give you." From his suit pocket, he pulled a rectangular black velvet jeweler's box and placed it in front of her.

Floored, Amanda stared at the box.

"Open it," he urged her.

Her heart pounding in her chest, she met his gaze and shook her head. "Why did you do this?"

"Because I wanted to thank you for all you've done for Lilly," he said. His green eyes deepened with passion. "And me. Open it."

Biting her lip, she opened the box. Nestled in the velvet lining lay a strand of pearls. Amanda's breath stopped. "They're beautiful," she said. "I—I—I don't know what to say. They're beautiful, but this is unnecessary. I adore Lilly, and you know how I feel about you, so—"

Jack gently squeezed her hand. "It's a gift, a thank-you. Accept it."

"I don't know how," she confessed in a whisper.

Jack's gaze grew gentle. He stood and walked behind her. "It's easy. You put on the pearls," he said, lifting the necklace from the box and fastening it around her neck. "Then you say 'They're beautiful. Thank you.'"

She swallowed a lump in her throat. "They're beautiful. Thank you."

He lowered his head to hers. "Then you kiss me."

She raised her lips to his. He made it so easy for her to forget that he wasn't in love with her.

Carol paid a surprise visit the following week after Amanda put Lilly down for a nap.

"The boss let us off early because we just finished a big project at work. I hadn't seen you in a while, so I thought I'd drop by. Very nice house," Carol said, looking around the formal living room. She grinned slyly. "I could be a nanny in these kind of surroundings."

"You'd last a day or two," Amanda said. "You're too independent."

She flopped onto a love seat. "I dunno. This is pretty nice. I like your hair."

"Thank you."

"Now, tell me everything."

Amanda quickly shared some of the recent events. "But he's not in love with me," she finished, wondering if she was warning herself as much as she was warning Carol.

Carol shook her head. "He doesn't love you? The

man has made love to you, given you pearls, taken you out to the best restaurant in Minneapolis and he doesn't love you?''

"Right," Amanda said.

"If he doesn't love you, then what does he feel for you?"

"He likes me," Amanda said, wincing at how lame that sounded. "He likes me intensely. Carol, mine isn't a face that would launch a thousand ships." She stood, restlessly adjusting a lampshade.

Carol sighed. "Most of us weren't born with a face that would launch a thousand ships. We just do the best with what we've got. I've always thought you hid your light under a bushel."

"What do you mean?"

"You're so quietly pretty. There's nothing wrong with that. But didn't you ever want to make a little noise with your appearance?"

"No," Amanda said, thinking she'd always stuck to tried-and-true conservative styles.

Carol groaned. "You always look like you're ready for an inspection from Social Services."

"I always had to be," Amanda said, remembering the scary years after her mother died.

"Well, you don't now."

Amanda frowned. "But my job—"

"You're a temporary nanny."

"But I will be a secretary."

"And you can wear a range of clothing. Besides, despite your previous misconceptions, aren't you more than your job?"

Amanda chewed her lip thoughtfully. "Yes."

"What are you thinking?"

"Chloe Fortune gave me the name of a spa that does makeovers. I let a stylist trim my hair a couple of weeks ago."

"It looks good," Carol said, nodding her head expectantly. "So?"

"So you're right. I don't have to face Social Services anymore. Maybe it's time for me to have a makeover."

"Hallelujah!" Carol said.

Amanda looked askance at her friend. "There is such a thing as too much enthusiasm right now."

Carol rubbed her hands together. "This is gonna be so much fun. You *must* take pictures. You must share them with me."

"I don't know if the spa takes pictures."

"I don't mean pictures of you. I mean pictures of Jack when he sees you." She laughed. "I can't wait. When he finds out you've done a makeover for him, he will be on his knees."

Amanda shook her head. "I can't imagine Jack on his knees. That won't happen," she assured Carol. "Besides, I'm not getting this makeover for Jack."

Carol wrinkled her brow. "Then who are you getting it for?"

Amanda thought of all the years she'd done everything she could to keep her family together. Dressing and acting older had begun as a necessity, then turned into a habit. Her life was different now, her responsibilities were different. She smiled at Carol. "I'm getting it for me."

Ten

Lilly accompanied Amanda to The Red Carpet Spa and Salon. While Jacques wrapped strands of Amanda's hair in foil, Amanda read *The Little Engine That Could* to Lilly. Then Gina gave Amanda a facial and cosmetic application. The good-natured makeup artist powdered Lilly's nose and put lipstick on her little mouth. Sheer indulgence or insanity drove Amanda to spring for a manicure for Lilly at the same time she got a French manicure.

The wardrobe consultant failed to conceal a slight grimace at Amanda's plain dress and offered several suggestions from the adjoining fashionable boutique. Amanda bought one outfit from head to toe, along with two dresses and the most romantic nightgown she'd ever seen.

Although she bit her tongue at the hem length of

the suit and the heels were taller than she usually bought, when Amanda looked in the mirror, she almost didn't recognize herself. Her hair was lit with gold highlights, and a long bang curved over one well-groomed eyebrow. Her eyes looked large and alluring, her mouth full and sensual. In the suit, stockings and heels, her body was slim, youthful and sexy.

Sexy? Her?

Amanda blinked.

The wardrobe consultant insisted Amanda wear the sophisticated pink plaid boucle suit out the door. With Lilly skipping along beside her, they walked two blocks to Fortune headquarters. The man in front of her held the door and smiled at her. She waved at the security attendant for the elevators for Kate Fortune's cosmetic company, and he looked slightly bemused as if he couldn't quite place her.

Another man held the elevator for Lilly and her, and introduced himself before he got out.

Jack's assistant did a double take. "You look terrific," Elaine said. "Go on in."

"Thanks," Amanda said and led Lilly through Jack's office door. He was talking with Ned Vandergrift, his top manager. When Jack saw her, he stopped mid-sentence and silence descended.

Amanda almost didn't believe it, but Jack Fortune's stubborn jaw dropped and it was clear he was momentarily speechless. Feeling a sudden attack of nerves, Amanda rushed to fill the conversational lull. "Sorry we're a few minutes late. I hope it's not a problem."

"Amanda?" Ned said in disbelief. "You look terrific. Nannyhood must agree with you. Jack was just telling me about your temporary assignment.''

''Thank you.''

''Will you be coming back to the office anytime soon?''

Amanda looked at Jack and saw his mouth tighten. ''That's yet to be determined,'' he said. ''We can finish this afternoon, Ned. Does three o'clock work for you?''

Ned nodded. ''No problem. See ya then,'' he said and winked at Amanda. ''You're gonna cause some neck strain today. Goddess material,'' he whispered as he walked past her.

Amanda felt her cheeks heat and welcomed turning the attention to Lilly. ''Show your daddy your pretty fingernails,'' she said.

Lilly held up her hands and wiggled her fingers. ''I got powder and lipstick, too,'' she said proudly puckering her lips.

Jack smiled and bent down to kiss her forehead. ''So you did, gorgeous.''

Lilly pranced off to admire herself in his mirror.

He straightened and held Amanda with his gaze. ''What have you done to herself?''

By the tone of his voice, she couldn't be sure if he was pleased or not. ''It's called a makeover. I went to The Red Carpet Spa.''

''Why?'' he asked. ''You were fine before.''

Fine. What a lukewarm description. She smiled. ''I guess I wanted to be more than fine for at least a day,'' she said. ''It's kinda fun. Some people haven't recognized me. Lunch should be interesting. Carol's taking me to lunch at The Brewery.''

Silence followed. "The Brewery," he repeated, struggling to keep the disapproval from his voice. The trendy, casual restaurant was a white-collar meat market. Amanda would be walking into a pack of hungry wolves.

"Well, you haven't said anything," she said expectantly, unclasping her hands and sweeping them outward. "What do you think?"

"The skirt is too short, the suit hugs your body. Your hair and eyes—" He stopped and swore under his breath. Her eyes sparkled seductively and her mouth could launch a dozen erotic dreams. He'd decided Amanda was quietly sexy, but this had definitely turned up the volume. "You look good enough to eat. I'm thinking of confining you to your room," he said, pulling her toward him. "No, make that my room."

He kissed her and felt a hint of new boldness in her response. A kick of arousal ran through his veins. Her tongue swept over his before she pulled back, self-consciously licking her lips. "I forgot about Lilly."

So had he. "I'm not sure I should let you out in public. Some guy on the street could get hurt looking at you instead of watching where he's going."

Her eyelashes swept downward shielding her gaze from him. "You're so amusing."

"I'm not joking," he said. "Are you shopping?"

Amanda shook her head. "I did enough of that this morning."

"For a man," Jack said.

Her eyes widened in genuine surprise. "When I'm involved with you?" she asked in disbelief. "I know we don't have any kind of agreement or anything, but—'' She sighed. ''I'm sure it's not wise to feed your ego, but you put them all in the shade. I'll probably regret saying that, but it's done,'' she said cheerfully. ''I need to run. I'll see you in about an hour. Have fun with your princess.''

With a tinge of unease, he watched her walk out of his office, appreciating the feminine sway of her hips and her long, silky legs. Every guy in The Brewery would be watching her the same way he was. Possessiveness surged through him. He stifled the ridiculous urge to call security and send an escort with her.

Before, he'd considered Amanda safe from being propositioned overly much. Although she was pretty, she did little to emphasize her attributes. Plus, she'd admitted she was in love with him. The combination had made him comfortable, perhaps too comfortable. He frowned.

Lilly tugged at his hand. ''I'm hungry. Let's eat.''

''Okay,'' he said, allowing her to lead him to the table set up in his office for their lunch. ''Did you have fun with Amanda this morning?''

Lilly nodded. ''She read me books while a man put her hair in Christmas paper.''

Jack's lips twitched at Lilly's version of the experience.

''Some men on the street made whistle noises at her. She didn't hear 'em, but I did.'' Lilly picked up her sandwich and paused. ''She's a good nanny. I want to keep her.''

Jack heard the longing behind the demand in his daughter's voice. He wanted to keep Amanda, too.

* * *

After they tucked Lilly in early that night, Jack chuckled at Amanda and pulled her into his arms. She was still in her makeover clothes. "Have you enjoyed yourself today? Turning half of Minneapolis on their ears," he said.

"Only half?" she asked in mock wide-eyed innocence.

"The other half didn't see you," he grumbled.

"It was interesting," she confided. "I've never done the 'babe' thing before."

"Uh-oh," he said. "Has The Red Carpet Spa created a monster?"

She lifted her shoulders in a shrug and smiled. "I don't know. I guess you'll have to stay tuned."

He would, Jack thought. "I wonder if you'll remember who knew you were a babe before the makeover," he mused.

"Who is that?"

"Me," he said, clenching his jaw.

"Oh," she said. "I could've sworn you said I looked 'fine.'"

"Nothing's wrong with fine," he said.

"How would you like it if the stockholders described your performance as VP of marketing as fine?"

Jack immediately rebelled at the thought. *"Fine?"*

"Kinda lukewarm and boring term, isn't it?" she said, wrinkling her nose and smiling at the same time.

Jack frowned. She had misunderstood him. "You're not lukewarm or boring. You have a quiet beauty."

Her eyes gentled. "That is lovely, Jack. I appre-

ciate it,'' she said, then kissed his cheek. ''But there
are times when every women wants to knock men off
their feet.''

He nodded slowly and squeezed her waist. He
would be a fool to underestimate her appeal. ''You
can knock one man off his feet tonight.''

''How's that?'' she asked, her voice threaded with
subtle sensuality.

''Come to my room.''

Her gaze glinted with uncertainty and she looked
away, lifting her hand to his chest. ''How about if
you come to my room?''

He felt a bittersweet mix of regret and tenderness.
She would make love with him, but she didn't want
to return to his bed where she had first given herself
to him. He had insulted her. He kissed her forehead,
resolved. She would come to his bed again. Not tonight, but soon.

The following day, three managers stopped by
Jack's office to tell him they'd heard Amanda was
going to be reassigned and each would be pleased to
have her as his assistant. If that weren't enough, when
he arrived home the phone rang several times—men
asking for Amanda. By the end of the evening Jack
was drinking a double scotch as he paced his study.

He wasn't VP of marketing just for show at Fortune. He understood supply and demand. There were
many men and one Amanda. It was time to take her
off the market.

That evening, Amanda was exhausted. Lilly was
clearly coming out of her shell. It was bedtime, and
the little girl had the giggles and asked for one more

book three times. Amanda relented until the last. "You read it to me," Amanda said, opening *Goldilocks and the Three Bears*.

"I can't read," Lilly protested.

"Look at the pictures and tell your own story," she said, falling back on Lilly's pillow and closing her eyes.

"Once upon a time, there was three bears and a girl named Goldilocks. She went 'sploring in the woods without her mother's permission and saw a house and went inside and ate yucky porridge because she was so hungry she didn't care what she ate."

Amanda chuckled. "Go girl."

"She ate the papa bear's porridge and it was *too* hot. She ate the mama bear's porridge and it was *too* cold. She ate the baby bear's porridge 'cause it was just right. 'Cept she wouldn't have eaten any of that yucky porridge if she'd had a peanut butter and jelly sandwich."

Amanda smiled as she listened to Lilly's little voice. Lord, she loved that child. She didn't know how she would be able to leave her, she thought, feeling her heart contract and her smile fade. It hurt to think of not tucking Lilly in at night, missing her sunny smile. She would even miss her prenap crabbiness.

"And when Goldilocks saw the three bears, she screamed bloody murder and ran all the way home."

Amanda felt Lilly's breath on her face, then her little finger gently pushed at her eyelid. Amanda caught her hand and Lilly squealed.

"It's time for you to go to sleep," Amanda said, "so I can, too."

Lilly sighed and slid under the covers and hugged Amanda's neck tightly. "You're the best nanny in the world. I want you to stay forever."

Amanda's chest tightened. She hugged Lilly and fought the sting of tears. "You're the best little girl in the world," Amanda said. "Sweet dreams, sweetheart. Your daddy will kiss you after he gets home."

Sighing, she glanced up and caught sight of Jack beside the bed. His gaze felt strangely ominous.

"Daddy's here now," he murmured, then bent down to kiss his daughter. "Good night, princess."

He wrapped his hand around Amanda's and led her out the door. "I need to talk to you. Let's go to the study."

"Okay." She studied his solemn expression and felt her stomach dip. "Sounds serious."

He nodded. "It is."

They took the rest of the short walk sans conversation. The sound of his hard-soled leather shoes on the hardwood hall floor downstairs heightened her tension. She had seen Jack this way on very few occasions—during his divorce and when his wife died. Frayed around the edges from her long, busy day, Amanda considered asking for a rain check. She wondered if she might do better with a nap and cookies before she faced this.

Jack released her hand as they entered the study. She bit her lip.

"Have a seat," he said, his voice quiet.

Amanda gingerly lowered herself to the love seat and folded her hands in her lap. She looked expectantly at Jack.

He looked away and began to pace.

"I've thought about this a lot. I think it's the best plan for all the parties involved."

Amanda nodded, but she didn't have a clue what he was talking about.

"Lilly needs a permanent female figure in her life. She needs more than a nanny. I respect you and care for you. I admire you," he said, and cleared his throat. He raked his hand through his hair. "My attorney advises a prenuptial agreement. I assure you it will be fair. You'll be taken care of regardless of any eventualities, and you would have all the benefits of the Fortune name."

Amanda's brain locked up on *prenuptial agreement.*

"I want you to be my wife and Lilly's mother," Jack said, pulling a jeweler's ring box from his pocket. He opened it, and a large oval diamond flashed in the light. "Will you marry me?"

Amanda felt as if she were hanging upside down from the top of the Ferris wheel. Certain her heart and lungs had stopped functioning, she stared blankly at Jack.

He waved his hand in front of her face. "Amanda, did you hear me?"

She blinked and took a shaky breath. "Pardon?"

"I asked you to marry me," he said.

Amanda caught sight of the ring and gulped. Bowing her head, she rubbed her forehead, wishing she could clear her head. "I—uh—I'm so surprised," she said. *What an understatement.* She wasn't certain her heart was working yet.

"I can see that," he said, amusement slipping into his deadly serious tone. He gently moved her hand away from her eyes and met her gaze. "Amanda, I think we can all be good for each other. We can have a good life together."

Amanda nodded. Everything Jack had said played through her mind. Lilly, marriage, prenuptial agreement, respect, care, admire.

But not love.

Her heart fell in disappointment. He wanted marriage, part of her argued. That meant something. That meant she was special to him.

But not love.

This was an unproposal. She glanced at the ring, pulled back her hand and sighed. "I'd like to think about it."

Surprise crossed Jack's face. "You want to think about it," he repeated.

She nodded.

"You want to think about it."

"If that's okay," she said.

"Yes," he said in an unconvincing voice. "Of course it's okay." He snapped the ring box closed and nodded. "You think about it."

She forced her lips to approximate a smile. "Thank you." She stood, clasping her hands together. "I'll think about it. Good night."

Amanda put one foot in front of the other. She climbed the stairs and went to her room. She stood in the dark for five seconds, then ran to the bathroom and lost her dinner. Amanda rinsed her mouth and held a cool washcloth to her face while she sat on the edge of the tub.

The man she loved, her dream man, the man who put every other man in the shade for her, had just asked her to marry him. If she ignored his lack of emotion, it would have been a dream come true. She had the chance to spend the rest of her life as his wife. She could be euphoric.

If he loved her.

Amanda's hands trembled. She thought of Lilly, and her heart clenched. Maybe Jack would grow to love her, she thought, and wondered if it was dangerous to hope. She loved him. She wanted him happy and fulfilled, and if she could be a part of that, she couldn't imagine being happier herself. If he didn't love her, though, wouldn't he ultimately grow tired of her?

Amanda thought of Jack's somber attitude when he'd proposed to her. She'd watched him deliver sales presentations with more enthusiasm.

She buried her face in her hands. Heaven help her, she didn't know what to do.

Eleven

Amanda brooded over Jack's unproposal for the next few days. When he arrived home at night, she felt him watching her, waiting silently. The more she thought about it, the more she sadly concluded that marrying Jack might very well not make him happy.

Although her heart rebelled at the idea of denying him or Lilly something so important, she knew Jack saw their marriage more as a business deal. His unproposal would likely lead to an unmarriage. She didn't want that for herself or Jack.

With each passing day the tension in the house mounted. Although Jack knew it was best from a negotiational stance for Amanda to come to him, her evasiveness stuck in his craw. The woman loved him, for Pete's sake. The decision should have been a snap for her.

After a week Jack confronted her in the hallway just after she came out of the bathroom. She wore a short white nightgown that reminded him of her innocence. Her eyes widened in surprise at the sight of him.

"Hi," she said in a quiet voice.

"I'd like us to talk," he said in the most reasonable tone he could muster. "My bedroom or yours?"

She was silent for so long he wondered if she would refuse. "Mine," she finally said.

He closed her bedroom door behind him and leaned his back against it. Crossing his arms over his chest, he drank in the sight of her, surprised at how much he'd missed her.

"You want to know my answer, don't you?" she asked, standing on the opposite end of the room.

"Yes." His gut twisted at the indecision in her voice.

"Well, your proposal was very generous, but I'd like to make a counteroffer."

Suspicion trickled through his veins like poison. Did she want more assurance of money? The thought brought a bitter taste to his mouth. "What's that?"

She shrugged her shoulders. "Why don't we just live together for a while?"

Floored, Jack stared at her, speechless for a long moment. He shook his head. "Part of the purpose of the marriage is to provide a permanent, stable relationship for Lilly, you and me."

"But you don't really want to marry me, Jack," Amanda said quietly.

"That's not true." Unable to remain still, he pushed away from the door. *Why* was this woman arguing with him? He would never have anticipated this in a million years. He'd thought Amanda was thoroughly traditional in her attitude toward marriage. "I have carefully considered this and think it's the best option for all the parties involved."

Amanda nodded and gave a sad smile. "Option, parties. This sounds like a business deal."

Jack felt a twinge of discomfort, but brushed it aside. "In some ways marriage is," he said. "There are legal issues, financial issues, responsibilities—"

Amanda held up her hand and shook her head. "Maybe they're not necessary in this situation. Maybe we should just live together for a while."

Frustrated, Jack took a long breath and tried to hold onto his patience. "Lilly loves you. She needs—"

"Lilly is going to be fine," Amanda said. "She went to her play group today and stayed the entire time without me. Lilly is healing." She sighed. "Jack, it would be stupid for me to marry you when you don't really want to get married. We would both end up miserable."

"If I didn't want to marry you, I'll be damned if I would ask you. I've already been through one hellacious marriage. I don't want to go through another."

Silence settled between them like the soft whisk of a curtain lowering. "You shouldn't go through another marriage with that attitude," she told him. Her words were blunt, but her tone was soft. "You sounded positively funereal when you proposed to me."

Jack felt his jaw tighten. "Marriage is serious business."

Amanda rolled her eyes. "But it doesn't have to mean death." She walked toward him and lifted her hand to touch his arm. "Why would I want to marry you when you don't love me?"

She was confusing the hell out of him. "Some women would appreciate my financial resources. Some would enjoy the influence of the Fortune name. Some women might not find me objectionable as a husband," he said, unable to keep the sarcasm from his voice.

"Well, more than anything this woman wants you to be happy. I'm not convinced that marrying me will accomplish that."

Jack's head began to pound. He met her gaze. It was all perfectly clear to him. "Lilly needs you in her life. I want you. You love me. We should be married."

Amanda's eyes were sad. "I'm sorry."

Jack's disappointment was a crushing weight in his chest. "Does this mean you're leaving?"

"Not immediately, unless that's what you want," Amanda said.

"No," Jack quickly said.

"It needs to be done gradually. I thought it would be best to find another nanny and perhaps just have her come a couple of days a week while I'm still here. I'd like Lilly to spend some more time with your mother to strengthen that tie. Lilly has asked to visit her mother's grave, so—"

Jack's stomach turned. "I don't want her focusing on Sandra. I don't want her thinking about her."

Amanda looked at him in disbelief. "Sandra was her mother, so she's going to think about her. Lilly has to grieve in her own way."

"Sandra is gone, and Lilly needs to move on."

"She will," Amanda said. "On her own timetable."

"I don't want—"

"You're wrong about this," Amanda said firmly. "*You* need to get over Sandra. You need to get past your bitterness. If you can't do it for yourself, then you need to do it for your daughter. You may hate Sandra for what she did to you, but that doesn't change the fact that she was the mother of your child."

Beyond his anger and frustration, he heard the truth in what Amanda said. He didn't like it one damn bit, but he heard it. He wanted to punch the wall. He wanted to yell, but how could he yell at her when she was right. He pointed his finger at Amanda. "You followed orders much better when you were my assistant in the office."

"You gave me a job to do with Lilly, and I'm going to do it. I'm going to make sure she heals. She's getting stronger every day. She's happy, and she's going to be even happier."

Jack turned to Amanda. "If you want her happy, then you should marry me."

Amanda's eyes shiny with unshed tears, she stood on tiptoe and took his mouth with hers. She kissed him with sweet passion, then slowly pulled away. "I love you too much to marry you."

Jack leaned back in his desk chair and groaned. What a week. His marriage proposal had been rejected, he'd had to fire his marketing research manager and he'd just learned some disturbing news about his father's company. The only thing Jack wanted was to head for his cabin at the lake and lick his wounds.

His phone rang, and he scowled at it. He'd asked his assistant to hold all calls. "Jack Fortune," he said.

"Hello, Mr. Vice President," the rough, wry voice of his brother said.

Jack's crummy mood lifted a fraction. "Trade you a vice presidency with a view of Minneapolis for a ranching position in Wyoming."

"No room for former VPs at my Final Destination Ranch," Garrett said. "I got your message. Rough day?"

"Yeah, I found out Gray McGuire has acquired enough Knight Star stock to do some serious damage to Dad's company."

Garrett gave a low whistle. "That's bad news. Have you told Dad yet?"

"I will later. I wanted to call you first. I don't know what McGuire's agenda is."

"Keep me posted. By the way, how's the woman in your life?"

"Don't ask," Jack said.

"What's wrong with Lilly?"

Jack paused.

"Wrong woman?" he asked with far too much brotherly intuition.

"Right woman, for a change. I asked Amanda to marry me."

"That's great news. I wondered if you would ever take the plunge—"

"She turned me down, Garrett." Jack felt the return of his headache and pinched the bridge of his nose.

Silence followed.

Jack heard Garrett's muffled chuckle and pulled the phone away from his ear to stare at the handset. He thought about hanging up, but returned the phone to his ear.

"Amanda said no," Garrett said and chuckled again. "She's smarter than I thought."

"Keep it up, bro, and you'll bc listening to Mr. Dial Tone."

"Okay. It wouldn't be funny if I wasn't sure you were going to help her change her mind."

Something inside him eased a bit. "Thanks for the vote of confidence," he said.

"You sound worried. Closing is your specialty."

"Usually," he conceded. "But not this time. She said she loved me too much to marry me."

"That's original. How did you present the idea to her?"

Jack felt a surge of discomfort. "You have to remember that my relationship with Amanda began professionally. We didn't have the usual hearts and flowers," he said, thinking his heart was locked up.

"You didn't try to sell this as a business arrangement, did you?"

Jack hesitated.

"Oh, Jack, you should know better."

"I pointed out the financial and security advantages of marrying me,'' he said, hating the defensiveness in his voice.

"And?"

"And she suggested we live together," Jack said in distaste. The memory drove him nuts. He had to stand.

"Sounds like she doesn't want your money," Garrett mused.

"No."

"Sounds like she doesn't give a rip about getting the Fortune name or image."

"No."

"Sounds like a winner to me. Just like I found."

"Yes," Jack said, and he had to find a way to get her.

By the time he arrived home that evening, it was well past Lilly's bedtime. Weary, he slipped into her room and kissed her forehead. For a satisfying, timeless moment, he watched her even breathing and her sweet, sleep-flushed cheeks. He walked out of her bedroom, noticed there was no light from beneath Amanda's door and headed for his own room.

Tired and discouraged, he started to push open his door when he noticed the light was on. He frowned and walked into his room, immediately spotting a goddess on his bed.

"I missed you," she said with a secret smile.

Her hair was tousled and sexy, her gaze welcoming and intent on him. She wore a silky apricot negligee that was so pretty he didn't know whether he wanted her to leave it on or take it off. Amanda in tigress mode.

The bitter taste of the day faded. Just looking at her renewed him. He walked toward her. "What a—" He stopped, almost saying the word *nice*. He didn't want to understate her effect. "Spectacular surprise."

Her smile broadened and she raised up on her knees, pressing the pearls he'd given her to her lips.

He toyed with one of her shoulder straps. "This is so pretty I hate to take it off," he said. "But I will."

She unknotted his tie. "I always thought you looked great in a suit."

Approving her boldness, he watched the fire in her eyes. "You did?"

"Uh-huh, and I wondered how you looked out of your suit."

"And?" he prompted as she unbuttoned his shirt.

"You take my breath away."

His blood heated his skin, and his heart rate picked up. He ditched his shirt and kicked off his shoes. She tugged him toward her and kissed him, a tenderly carnal caress. Her hands skimmed over his chest and ribs. He could feel a sexual buzz emanating from her skin. She wanted to consume him. The knowledge made him hard.

Her tongue cupping and sucking his, she unfastened his slacks and pushed them down. Jack pushed down the straps of her gown, and her breasts brushed his chest.

Her hair was silk in his fingers, her mouth an instrument of sensual devotion. "I want to make love to you all night long," he muttered against her lips.

She shook her head, sliding her hands over his hips.

"No?"

Amanda pulled back slightly and brought her hands to the front of his thighs. She caressed him intimately, and Jack groaned at the sensation.

"I want to make love to you tonight."

She continued stroking him. "No argument here," he said, his voice rough to his own ears.

"Good," she said, loving him with her eyes before she took him into her mouth.

"Oh, Amanda." The pleasure was so intense he swore under his breath. "I can't stand much more."

She pulled away, her gaze sultry. "I want you," she whispered, pulling him down with her on the bed, "every way."

Rolling onto his back, he tugged her on top of him filling his hands with her tight, sweet bottom. Her sexy scent made him crazy. Finding her wet and wanting, he played with her femininity, feeling her grow swollen beneath his touch.

Her moan touched off every male nerve ending in his body. He wanted to possess and be possessed. He dipped his finger inside her at the same time he slid his tongue into her mouth. She strained and arched against him.

Her legs parted and he positioned himself between them. She rippled back and forth against his aching hardness, bringing him close to her delicious opening, then moving away.

Jack began to sweat. Amanda arched against him. She moved her pelvis in a mesmerizing searching motion. "Inside," she said. "I want you inside."

Sucking in a deep breath, he slowly thrust inside her. Wet and tight. Her eyes closed for a second and she shuddered around him. Then she looked at him with such a powerful passion that he could have lost himself in her. When she began to ride him, he did just that.

In fluid mind-robbing motions, she pumped him, lifting his hands to cup her swollen breasts. Her eyes didn't leave his face as she drove him on. The sight of her naked swaying body made his mouth dry, but it was the pleasure on her face that sent the first ripples of climax through him.

Through the haze of his intense desire, he could see that her pleasure didn't come just from how they made love—it was far more personal. The turn-on for Amanda centered on him. He'd never known such intimacy, and it shot his control to hell and back.

"I love you," she said, shattering around him in completion.

He felt her words to the core, and thrust deep inside her in a long, scalding release. Amanda sank down on top of him, tucking her head in his shoulder, her breath coming in soft pants on his skin.

Jack closed his arms around her, holding her close. A few moments passed before he found his wits. "Marry me," he whispered in her ear. "I want you here every night."

She groaned and put her hand over his mouth. "Stop tempting me. You turn my body into an earthquake and now you're trying to catch me at a weak moment."

"Is it working?"

She groaned again.

"Is that the secret? Tempting you until you say yes?"

She pulled back slightly and lifted her hand to his chin. The devotion and sadness in her eyes created a unique pain in his chest. "I think you know what the secret is."

Jack felt his stomach sink. She wanted him to love her. She wanted the one thing he couldn't give her because another woman had left his heart with a barbwire fence around it.

Twelve

In the early hours before dawn, Jack made love to Amanda again. The strength of his desire took her breath, and she felt herself sinking more deeply in love with him. It frightened her. Long moments afterward Amanda still trembled. She felt incredibly vulnerable.

"I should go," Amanda said. "Lilly could wake up early."

"So?" Jack said, tightening his arms around her as if he had no intention of letting her leave.

"So it might be tough explaining why Amanda is in Daddy's bed."

"You can tell her we're living together," he said in a silky voice. "Wasn't that your counteroffer?"

Surprised, Amanda felt a rush of butterflies in her stomach. Jack had been so adamant that she hadn't believed he would take her up on the counteroffer. "I—uh—"

"It might be a good idea after all," Jack said. "It's a very successful marketing technique. For a limited time, the customer tries out the product, and if they don't return it, the product becomes theirs permanently." He gave a dangerous grin. "You can try me on for a while and see if I'm good husband material."

Uh-oh. She'd heard that tone in his voice before, right before he bagged a major account. Amanda gulped. "I'm not sure—"

"You're not reneging, are you?"

Yes, her survival instincts screamed, but she couldn't turn down the challenge in his eyes. "No," she said, wondering what she was getting herself into.

He slid out of bed and stood naked in front of her. He extended his hand to her. "Take a shower with me."

Her heart dipped, and she stared at him. "A shower," she repeated weakly.

"C'mon. Find out if I'm any good in the shower," he challenged.

Amanda accepted his invitation to lead her into his bathroom and quickly learned she was in big trouble. She couldn't recall much soaping and scrubbing. Instead, she remembered the sensation of Jack's slick skin against hers, incredible pleasure...and sighs, gasps and whispered oaths.

Later that afternoon her favorite flowers, sweetheart roses, arrived with a message from Jack: "Thank you for a wonderful night. It could be every night..."

Her heart twisted at the possibility. Deep down,

Amanda knew, however, that if Jack didn't truly love her, his passion for her would fade. Then what would they have? She couldn't bear the idea of becoming invisible to him again.

Over the next few days Jack seemed determined to obliterate that thought from her mind. He took her to his bed every night and called every day from work. He sent her fresh strawberries, her favorite fruit, and Amanda grew curious about where he was getting his information about her. She'd never told him she loved strawberries.

When she asked him, he just smiled and said, "A husband knows these things."

Despite the fact that Jack was chipping away at her resolve, Amanda continued with her plans for Lilly. After a trip to Sandra's grave site, she and Lilly met Marie for lunch on her patio overlooking the gardens and the lake.

"Your flowers are beautiful," Amanda said.

"Thank you. Gardening has always been a comfort for me. You can pick a few flowers, darling," Marie said to Lilly. "The purple pansies right over there and the red ones right next to them." She put her arm around Lilly and pointed out the flowers.

Marie watched Lilly skip away and sighed, then glanced at Amanda. "I can't tell you how much it means to be able to see Lilly. I never understood why Sandra kept her away from Jack," she said, then frowned. "Well, maybe I do understand. I'm not sure Sandra ever really loved Jack. Certainly not the way he needed to be loved. I think she may have been more interested in the monetary benefits of marrying a Fortune. That marriage was a point of honor for him, so he was wounded when it didn't work out. Such a sad time for him.''

Amanda remembered how she'd caught Jack staring at a picture of Lilly with such longing it had hurt to see it. "Yes, it was.''

"That's right," Marie said. "You worked for Jack during that difficult period. Things are very different now, thank goodness. Does he know you're in love with him?''

Amanda's lemonade went down the wrong way, and she choked. She coughed. "What makes you say that?''

"My dear, it's so obvious.''

Amanda sighed. "Unfortunately it's not reciprocal.''

Marie knit her brows in confusion. "Are you quite sure?''

Amanda felt a sliver of doubt. He had been so attentive and generous, so passionate. Maybe he did love her...maybe. She reminded herself that for all Jack had done, he'd never said the words. "Yes, I'm sure.''

Marie looked skeptical. "I think you two would do well together." She lifted her hand when Amanda opened her mouth to protest. "Don't mistake me for Kate. But I know what Jack has gone through. A mother can hope," she said with a gentle smile.

Amanda's problem was that with each passing day, she was hoping more and more that a miracle would happen and Jack would love her. Then she wouldn't have to go away.

It had been an evening of tears and temper. Lilly had missed her nap, and Miss Annabelle was missing.

The three-year-old petted Delilah while she and Amanda looked out Amanda's bedroom window at the stars.

Amanda stroked Lilly's hair. "Did you pick out your lucky star?"

Lilly nodded and pointed at the sky. "Right there. It's the brightest one."

"Have you made a wish?"

Lilly nodded again. "I wish we could find Miss Annabelle, but if we can't, I wish Delilah could stay in my room again tonight."

Amanda smiled down at her. "I think Delilah would love to spend the night in your room tonight." The thought struck her that taking Delilah with her when she left would be one more loss for Lilly. Her protective instincts warred with her attachment to her pet. Delilah had been hers since she'd moved to Minneapolis. Still, Amanda would have to be careful when she left that she didn't undo all of Lilly's healing. She sighed and pushed back another emotional hurt.

"As long as it's okay with your daddy, Delilah can sleep in your room every night."

Lilly's eyes grew round. "Really?" She looked down at Delilah, purring contentedly in her arms, then looked back at Amanda. "Wow! The star worked. I already got one of my wishes."

Amanda hugged her. "Sometimes it's just fun to make wishes."

"Like playing the favorites game?" Lilly asked.

"Exactly."

"Then where's your star? And what's your wish?"

Amanda felt a bittersweet pang. She couldn't remember the last time she'd wished on a star and really meant it. Seeing life through Lilly's eyes had been such a gift. She would miss it terribly. She glanced up at the sky and located the star she'd wished on as a child. "There it is."

"What's your wish?" Lilly asked.

"I wish that someone would fall crazy in love with me," she said, and felt her cheeks heat at the truth of her wish. "And I wish Lilly would go to sleep now and dream wonderful dreams," she said quickly.

"Me, too," Jack said from the doorway.

Amanda felt her cheeks blaze even more at his presence. She hoped he hadn't heard her first wish.

"Hi, Daddy," Lilly said, wiggling to get under the covers. "I get to keep Delilah with me tonight. I've been on lots of adventures today."

Still in his suit, Jack walked into the room and smiled at her. "I went to Mommy's grave and put flowers on it," Lilly told him.

Amanda watched his jaw tighten. "You did?" he asked in a too-controlled voice, and gave Amanda a hard, questioning glance.

"Yes, and then I ate lunch with Nana and she let me pick flowers, and then I came home and swam and lost Miss Annabelle and picked out a lucky star."

"You've had a busy day."

Lilly nodded and lifted her arms to give him a hug. "You should pick out a lucky star, too."

"Tomorrow night," Jack said. "It's past your bedtime. Good night, princess."

Amanda dropped a kiss on her cheek and turned off the light. She followed Jack out the door.

"I thought I told you I didn't want her focusing on Sandra," Jack said as soon as they walked a few steps from Lilly's room.

His voice was so cold it chilled her. "I told you I intended to take her."

"And I told you I didn't want her there."

"Did you want to take her?" she asked, trying but failing to keep the frustration from her tone.

Surprise glinted in his eyes, then he narrowed his gaze. "She's only three. She doesn't need to be in a graveyard."

"She asked to go."

"I don't want you taking her there again. Sandra was a selfish, lying, mean-spirited woman."

"There must have been something good about her," Amanda countered. "You married her."

Jack looked as if she'd hit him. "She was pregnant with my child at the time." His jaw worked in frustration. "Do not take her to the cemetery again."

Amanda shook her head. "I can't promise that. It's not in Lilly's best interest."

"Amanda, this is not a negotiation."

Amanda had the sense that they were arguing about far more than a visit to Sandra's grave. She had the oddest feeling that she was fighting for something more important for Lilly, for Jack, maybe even herself.

"Then you might have to fire me," she said quietly.

Jack stared at her in shocked silence.

Amanda felt herself begin to tremble from the inside out, but she stiffened her spine. Even if he hated her for it, she had to tell him the truth. "Jack, what

Sandra did to you was terrible. She shouldn't have lied and taken advantage of you. She shouldn't have kept you from your child. She shouldn't have treated your heart so callously. It grieves me that she did these things to you.'' It hurt her to remember how much pain Jack had endured and tried to hide.

She took a deep breath. ''But Sandra is gone now. She can't hurt you anymore. If you don't forgive her, then you're hurting Lilly and yourself. If you don't forgive her, then I'm not sure you'll ever be able to love anyone again. In that case, who wins?''

His face tightened with anger. ''You've gone too far. This is none of your business. You don't know what you're talking about,'' he said, then turned his back on her and walked away.

Amanda walked to her room and collapsed on the bed. Her body still trembled. The cold fury on Jack's face cut her to the core. She knew she had offended him. At the same time, she knew she'd had to tell Jack the truth. It had taken every bit of her courage, and she feared it had cost her any chance she might have had with him.

Over the next few days it became apparent that Jack would not forgive her for confronting him. He didn't invite her to his bed, nor did he come to hers. There were no more flowers or strawberries or calls from work. In the evenings he was distantly polite to her, excusing himself to his study as soon as helped tuck in Lilly.

Although she'd known she was taking a terrible risk by defying him, his cold politeness was almost more than she could bear. Despite all her efforts to the contrary, deep in her heart of hearts, Amanda had secretly hoped Jack might come to love her. Every carefully neutral word he now uttered to her twisted the knife inside her a little more.

She was going to have to leave soon. Lilly would be able to handle it, she thought. The three-year-old wouldn't like it, but she was tough like her dad, and she would survive well. Delilah, Amanda thought wryly, would help soften the blow. One day during Lilly's nap, she called a reputable nanny-finder service.

Amanda had enjoyed her time with Lilly, but now, every minute was like gold. She drank in the sound of her wonderful childish laughter and squeals, cherished her cookie-and-purple-fruit-punch kisses, and stored the memories in her heart and mind.

After dinner and a dog-paddling lesson in the pool, she read Lilly her favorite books, then saw Jack at the bedroom door. Sensing he wanted to tell Lilly good-night by himself, she excused herself, but lingered in the doorway. She wasn't storing up memories just of Lilly. She was also storing last memories of the man she loved.

"Hi, Daddy," Lilly said.

"Hi, princess," Jack said. "Did you like swimming?"

"I'm still dog-paddling. 'Manda says she wants me to be water safe."

Jack nodded. "I do, too."

Amanda tensed as she saw him glance at Lilly's bedside table. She'd left out Sandra's picture and Lilly's special memory book.

"What's this?" he asked, picking up the book.

"It's my mem'ry book of Mommy," she said. "I like it better than visiting the cemetery. I draw pictures of Mommy and tell 'Manda stories about her, and she writes them down for me," she said, then gave a little-girl shrug. "It makes me feel better. 'Manda says Mommy will always be in my heart. 'Manda knows cuz her mommy died, too."

A long silence followed, and Amanda's heart twisted as she watched Lilly and Jack. Her eyes burned with unshed tears. She closed her eyes and prayed that Jack wouldn't turn away from Lilly now.

Slowly opening her eyes, she saw him flip through the pages of the memory book and sigh. He reached out to touch her cheek. "I can tell you a story about your mommy," he said.

Lilly lit up like a Christmas tree. "You can?"

He nodded. "When you were getting ready to be born, there was a snowstorm. Your mommy knew you were going to come out, so we had to go to the hospital so the doctor could help."

"Doctors like to help babies come out, don't they?" Lilly asked.

Jack chuckled. "Yes, they do. They like to get paid for it, too. On the way to the hospital we got stuck in the snow, and your mommy was afraid you were going to be born in the car."

Amanda listened carefully to his voice, but she heard no anger or bitterness. He continued to tell Lilly the story, a story precious to each child, of how they came into the world, and how excited Mommy and Daddy were. It was the most generous thing she'd ever known Jack to do.

She knew it wasn't easy for him, and she loved

him for it. Tears streamed down her cheeks. Jack and Lilly were going to be okay. She could see it; she could feel it in her heart. They would be okay, but she wasn't so sure Amanda would be.

Jack didn't come to her that night, and he maintained his polite distance the next day. Knowing she couldn't stand it much longer, Amanda made plans to give Jack her notice the following week. Without revealing that it was her birthday, she asked Jack if she could have Saturday off. He declined, saying his parents were holding a gathering at their house and they'd requested her presence.

Amanda didn't argue because she had always celebrated her birthday quietly. Her tradition usually included lunch with a friend and a phone call with her brother and sisters.

On Saturday morning Lilly ran into her bedroom and bounced up and down on Amanda's bed.

"Good morning!" Lilly said, and kissed her.

Amanda's heart caught, and she smiled. "Good morning to you. You woke up happy."

Lilly nodded and giggled. "Uh-huh."

"Are you excited about going to Nana's today?"

Lilly nodded again and clamped her hand over her mouth.

Amused and confused by her attitude, Amanda tugged at Lilly's hand. "What's up with you, princess?"

Lilly clamped her other hand over her mouth and shook her head.

Jack poked his head in the open doorway and lifted

an eyebrow. "Would you like to watch some cartoons this morning, Lilly?"

"Yes," Lilly said, darting out of Amanda's room.

Amanda tentatively met Jack's gaze. "She's in a good mood."

"She is," he agreed. "How are you this morning?"

"Fine," Amanda said, trying to read his mood. "And you?"

"Hopeful," he said, his gaze quietly intent. "I'm fixing Belgian waffles. Join us?"

She stared at him in surprise. "Belgian waffles?" she repeated.

He nodded. "With strawberries."

A thousand questions raced through her mind. He didn't look angry or indifferent or the least bit cold. She felt the return of butterflies to her stomach. Dressed casually in jeans and an unbuttoned shirt, he looked at her with almost a tender hunger. Or maybe he just wanted breakfast, she thought, reining in her imagination.

"That sounds nice," she finally said. "I didn't know you could cook."

"Ah," he said with a slight, sexy grin. "Something you didn't know about me. Maybe you should stick around and see if there's anything else you don't know," he said, and headed down the hall.

Amanda stared after him in complete confusion. *Big* change, she thought of Jack. She narrowed her eyes. He couldn't know this was her birthday. He'd never noticed it before. Scratching her head, she eliminated that possibility and shrugged. She didn't know what had brought about the change.

For today, maybe she should simply enjoy it. It wasn't as if he was going to declare his love for her. He was just fixing waffles.

Breakfast was delicious. Jack was attentive. Lilly couldn't sit still in her seat and kept clamping her hand over her mouth. Jack encouraged her to watch more cartoons.

After breakfast, Amanda tried to call her brother and sisters, but none were at home. She pushed aside her twinge of disappointment and took a bath and helped Lilly get ready for the gathering at Jack's parents' house. After they pulled to a stop at the end of the Fortunes' drive, Marie greeted them while they were still in the car.

"Welcome. Welcome. It's so good to see you," Marie said. "Lilly, sweetheart, come and give your nana a hug."

Lilly practically leaped out of the car and skipped alongside Marie.

"I can't remember seeing her this squirmy," Amanda said.

Jack gave a half grin. "She's excited," he said, and decided to take advantage of a few moments alone with Amanda. In the past forty-eight hours, he'd faced several hard truths about himself, and Amanda was at the center of most of them. He took her hand. "Sometimes an apology isn't enough. I've been trying to find the right words."

"What do you mean?"

He looked into her understanding eyes and thanked God she hadn't left before he'd straightened himself out. He still wasn't sure she would forgive him. "I took my leftover anger at Sandra out on you. It was wrong. You don't deserve that.'' He shook his head. ''You know, I thought you were this quiet, conservative, agreeable woman. I was wrong about that, too. You've turned my world upside down, Amanda.'' He felt his gut knot with emotion. ''I'm sorry, and I know an apology isn't always enough.''

''It is with me,'' she whispered. ''I just want you to be happy, Jack.''

He closed his eyes, a sliver of relief sneaking in, although he knew all too well that she wasn't his yet. The last couple of days had turned him around, and everything was so much clearer to him. The time for hiding was done. ''You keep teaching me things about myself I didn't know. This won't happen again,'' he promised. ''I understand how important you are to me, and I want to make sure you know. I want you to know that—''

Lilly knocked on the car door window. She bounced up and down with excitement. ''Hurry up, Daddy! Everybody's waiting!''

Torn, Jack reluctantly nodded. ''We'll talk more later,'' he promised and kissed her. ''The princess is calling.''

He got out of the car and circled to her side to help Amanda out of her seat. She was starting to hope again, and that made her nervous.

With Lilly skipping along, they walked toward the garden. Lilly looked up at Jack. ''Now?''

He nodded and smiled. ''Now.''

''Happy birthday, 'Manda!'' Lilly yelled at the top of her lungs.

Blinking, Amanda felt Jack steer her around the corner to a group of people.

"Happy birthday, Amanda!"

The chorus stunned her. She caught a glimpse of her brother and sisters and Carol. Kate Fortune and other members of Jack's family rounded out the group. Overwhelmed, she could only gape.

"I was 'fraid the secret was gonna pop out, so Daddy told me to cover my mouth every time it wanted to pop out," Lilly said, pulling on Amanda's dress. "We're gonna have cake and ice cream."

"When did you do this?" she asked Jack.

"Two weeks ago," he told her, "I did some serious research on Amanda Corbain."

"Did you think about canceling when we—"

He put his fingers over her mouth and shook his head. "Never. I had to face some of my own demons, but I never wanted to lose you."

Her heart contracted. She had a dozen more questions for him, but her sisters rushed forward to hug her. The next few moments were a blur of hugs and sweet wishes. In the midst of it, Amanda was bowled over to learn that Jack had flown her brother and sisters to Minneapolis on the Fortune company jet and had wrangled information about her out of her siblings and Carol.

Marie gently but firmly urged everyone to the tables for a light luncheon. Amanda was certain the crêpes were delicious, but her taste buds must have been on strike due to shock. Her head was spinning from his apology. She'd almost given up. She couldn't believe Jack had arranged all this. No one had ever done anything like this for her before. It was the persistently compelling look in his eyes, however, that made every other beat of her heart stop.

When champagne was delivered with the cake, Jack stood and lifted his glass. "To Amanda, everyone here knows how special you are and all you do to make our lives better. I thank my lucky stars for the day you were born. Knowing you reminds me of the man I want to be. Happy birthday, sweetheart." He met her gaze directly. "I love you."

Distantly she heard the guests applaud, but for Amanda it was too many dreams coming true at once. She'd been swinging between doubt and despair too long. Her heart swelled in her chest. Amanda couldn't stop the tears sliding down her cheeks. Jack put his arms around her, and she sobbed.

"Sweetheart, what's wrong?" he asked, his voice full of concern.

"It's too much," she said. "Too much at once. Waffles would have been enough."

Jack looked at her in confusion. "Waffles?"

She nodded, sniffing. "Your apology, the party, and—" Her voice stopped. "You love me," she whispered. "Do you really love me?"

"More than you'll ever know," he said solemnly. "You saved my heart. You saved my life."

Epilogue

Three weeks later

Jack hadn't gained a reputation for being a great closer for nothing. He made it clear that while Amanda might have thought he was her big *Oh-no,* he was going to become her big *Oh-yes.* As soon as Amanda agreed to his marriage proposal, he told her he wanted her next words to be "I do."

That was why Amanda was currently ensconced on the balcony of a private villa and thanking her lucky star. It was also why she was wearing a negligee and a gold wedding band. She pinched herself, remembering that momentous day when he had given her his heart. Since then, their trust for each other had grown with each passing moment. She had thought she couldn't love him more, but she'd been wrong.

She had thought she knew everything about Jack, but he continued to give her new reasons to fall more deeply for him. Letting go of his hurt had truly freed him to love again.

Her heart swelled with emotion, and she sighed deeply.

She felt Jack step behind her and wrap his arms around her. His bare chest brushed her back. "Did I rush you?" he asked in a low voice that did delicious things to her nerve endings.

She smiled and turned in his arms. "Yes and no. I loved you for years when I was invisible."

He shook his head. "You weren't invisible. I was blind. Remember? You helped me see again." He kissed her, and she felt the sweet passion immediately surge between them.

He pulled back. "We could have waited if you'd wanted a larger wedding."

"We had a perfect wedding," she insisted. "Your mother was wonderful to allow the use of her garden again so soon after my birthday party."

"Some women would not be excited to see their stepdaughter pull out a bubble-making machine at the reception."

Amanda chuckled. "You did not marry one of those women," she told him, lifting her hand to his strong chin.

"Thank goodness," he murmured. "Isn't it time you were in bed?"

Her heart pounded at the look in his eyes. "Why?"

He cocked his head toward the sky. "It's my wish."

"Oh," she said. "I'm a big believer in wishes."

He lifted her in his arms and carried her to the bed, then followed her down. His body was warm and strong. He made her feel secure and aroused at the same time.

"You heard me that night I was wishing on a star, didn't you?" she asked.

"When you wished I would be as crazy for you as you were for me."

"I believe I said 'someone.'"

"You meant me," he told her, and she completely identified with his possessive tone. "It was easy for me to make that wish come true. As your husband, it's my job to make your wishes come true." He tugged the strap of her gown down with his teeth and blew his breath over her bare nipple. "Any other wishes?"

Her bones melted. "I wish you would kiss me."

He did, thoroughly.

"I wish you would love me forever," she said breathlessly.

"I will," he promised.

"And when we get back to Minneapolis," she said, sifting her fingers through the hair on his chest. "I wish you would make love to me on your desk."

Jack's eyes glinted with green fire. "Consider it done."

"But tonight I wish you would let me make you a little crazy," she said.

He rolled them both over so that she lay on top of him. "Now, you're making my wishes come true." His eyes made love to her. "But you've done that from the beginning."

*   *   *   *   *

*Find out what happens when Mollie Shaw finally
meets Gray McGuire in*

The Groom's Revenge
by
Susan Crosby

Available in June 2000.

Turn the page for a sneak preview…

———

No one will ever believe me, Mollie Shaw thought, shaking her head in disbelief. Gray McGuire, the high-tech wizard from the Silicon Valley was here. In her flower shop. He'd materialized from her dreams.

His blue eyes were startling against his Californian tan, his dark brown hair shiny and thick. The turquoise polo shirt and khaki pants he wore fit his body perfectly, showing off a well-toned physique, one that didn't look like he spent his days behind a desk.

Standing in front of her counter, her hands clasped, she was content to watch him. Afraid if she did something wrong, he would disappear in a puff of smoke. He'd certainly hightail it out of there faster than she could say, "You're the man of my dreams. Literally," if he caught a glimpse of the newspaper photograph of him she had taped to underneath her counter. She had even been talking to his picture when he'd arrived.

She continued to wait as he set some wind chimes moving then listened to the tinkling sounds.

She didn't want to hurry him, but she was more than a little curious about why he was there. Well, technically she was flabbergasted. But she was really, really curious. If this were a fairy tale, he'd be pulling a glass slipper out of his pocket now and trying it on her foot—and it would fit.

"It's a nice shop," he said at last. "You're also a wedding planner."

"How do you know that?"

He pointed to the left. "There's a sign in your window."

"Oh." She smiled, feeling a little sheepish. She'd thought maybe he was her soul mate, after all—that he could read her mind. "I'm just getting started. You know the Fortune family, right? I've heard them speak of you."

"You're friends with the Fortunes?" he asked, his expression impassive.

"My good friend Kelly married Mac Fortune, and I pulled the event together for them. Then I was invited to do Mac's sister Chloe's wedding to Mason Chandler in a few months. One of those fairy tale, princess weddings, with all the trimmings."

"The kind of wedding you'd like for yourself?"

She shrugged. "It's fun to plan, but it wouldn't be in my budget. My father's been gone since before I was born. My mother passed away last year."

Gray lifted his gaze in a flash when her words registered. Been gone? What did that mean? Was her father dead? "I'm sorry."

"Thank you. Now," she said glancing up at him, "what can I do for you, Mr. McGuire?"

"First you can call me Gray. I'm a little surprised you know me."

She fussed with a plant. "The Fortunes have spoken of you."

"But you recognized my face."

"I saw you on the news yesterday. What brings you to Every Bloomin' Thing?"

"I have a proposition for you."

"I hope I'm misunderstanding your meaning," Mollie finally said, her face growing red.

"Strictly business," he said gently before they were interrupted by a tiny, white-haired lady who'd come to get the church flowers.

Gray listened to the exchange between the women as they discussed the flower arrangements for church on Sunday. The conversation made him reconsider how far to involve her in his plans. He'd intended to align himself with her against Stuart Fortune. But this young woman seemed to live in a sheltered world that could not possibly have prepared her for launching a vendetta that would turn her into a media darling. Especially one born of an old scandal he would bring to light.

Mollie Shaw was a crucial component of Gray's plan to make Stuart Fortune's indiscretions and thievery public. But now that Gray had met this innocent young woman, how could he involve her?

How could he not? Justice must be rendered.

"I'm sorry for the interruption," Mollie said.

He looked around. They were alone again.

"You have a proposition for me?" she prompted him.

He had to rethink this. "I have to go. I'm expected somewhere else in a few minutes," he said, glancing at his watch, then heading for the door.

"Will you be back?"

Her words stopped him. There was something in her voice. A hopefulness he couldn't ignore. He didn't know what would happen next. He had to analyze—

"Please do come again," she said softly.

He should resist the temptation of her vulnerability, which whispered to his conscience first, then somewhere deeper, bringing light into the darkness of his plans—his need for vengeance. Instead he said, "I'll be in touch," over his shoulder as he moved to the door again.

* * *

Don't forget The Groom's Revenge
is on the shelves next month!

Sometimes bringing up baby can bring surprises –and showers of love! For the cutest and cuddliest heroes and heroines, choose the Special Edition™ book marked

That's my baby!

MAN OF THE MONTH

Look out for Desire's™ hottest hunks! Every month we feature our most sensual and sizzling man in a specially marked book.

SILHOUETTE
DESIRE
®

Men who can't be tamed by just *any* woman!

We know you'll love our selection of the most passionate and adventurous Sensation™ hero every month as the Heartbreaker.

Welcome back to the drama and mystery that is the Fortune Dynasty.

A Fortune's Children Wedding is coming to you at a special price of only £3.99 and contains a money off coupon for issue one of *Fortune's Children Brides*.

With issue one priced at a special introductory offer of 99p you can get it **FREE** with your money off coupon.

Published 24 March 2000

One-Off   The Hoodwinked Bride
         by Barbara Boswell   ISBN: 0 373 48378 3

No. 1   The Honour-Bound Groom
         by Jennifer Greene   ISBN: 0 373 76190 2

Published 21 April 2000

No. 2   Society Bride
         by Elizabeth Bevarly   ISBN: 0 373 76196 1

No. 3   The Secretary and the Millionaire
         by Leanne Banks   ISBN: 0 373 76208 9

Published 19 May 2000

No. 4   The Groom's Revenge
         by Susan Crosby   ISBN: 0 373 76214 3

No. 5   Undercover Groom
         by Merline Lovelace   ISBN: 0 373 76220 8

▼ SILHOUETTE
SPECIAL EDITION ®

AVAILABLE FROM 19TH MAY 2000

SHE'S HAVING HIS BABY Linda Randall Wisdom

That's My Baby!

Jake Roberts was everything Caitlin O'Hara wanted in her baby's father—he was fun, warm and gorgeous. They'd shared every intimate detail of their lives since childhood. Why not a baby?

A FATHER'S VOW Myrna Temte

Montana

Sam Brightwater wanted to start a traditional family. So the *last* woman he should be attracted to was Julia Stedman, who was only sampling her heritage. But Julia got under his skin and soon they were making love and making a baby…

BETH AND THE BACHELOR Susan Mallery

Beth was a suburban mother of two and her friends had set her up with a blind date—millionaire bachelor Todd Graham! He was sexy, eligible—everything a woman could want…

BUCHANAN'S PRIDE Pamela Toth

Leah Randall took in the man without a memory, but she had no idea who he was. They never planned to fall in love, not when he could be anyone…even one of her powerful Buchanan neighbours!

THE LONG WAY HOME Cheryl Reavis

Rita Warren had come home. She had things to prove. She didn't need a troublemaking soldier in her already complicated life. But 'Mac' McGraw was just impossible to ignore.

CHILD MOST WANTED Carole Halston

Susan Gulley had become a mother to her precious orphaned nephew, but she hadn't banked on falling for his handsome but hard-edged uncle. What would Jonah do when he learned the secret she'd been keeping?

AVAILABLE FROM 19TH MAY 2000

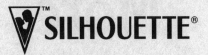

Intrigue
Danger, deception and desire

MIDNIGHT CALLER Rebecca York
HIS TO PROTECT Patricia Werner
UNDERCOVER DAD Charlotte Douglas
SECRET LOVER Shawna Delacorte

Desire
Provocative, sensual love stories

LEAN, MEAN AND LONESOME Annette Broadrick
LOVERS' REUNION Anne Marie Winston
SECRET BABY SANTOS Barbara McCauley
TAMING TALL, DARK BRANDON Joan Elliott Pickart
DAD IN DEMAND Metsy Hingle
ONE SMALL SECRET Meagan McKinney

Sensation
A thrilling mix of passion, adventure and drama

INVOLUNTARY DADDY Rachel Lee
EMILY AND THE STRANGER Beverly Barton
THE HORSEMAN'S BRIDE Marilyn Pappano
ANNIE AND THE OUTLAW Sharon Sala
HEARTBREAK RANCH Kylie Brant
AN OFFICER AND A GENTLE WOMAN
Doreen Owens Malek

0005/23b